Royalty may be al⋯
but sometimes carrying the hopes of your country
can be lonely. These two princes are about to
find their perfect princesses—and discover that
romance is the true power behind the throne.

WITHDRAWN

Raye Morgan
The Prince's Forbidden Love

and

Nina Harrington
The Ordinary King

in

Royal Wedding Bells

Praise for Raye Morgan

"Morgan's latest is a delightful reworking of a classic plot,
with well-drawn characters—particularly tortured hero Max—
and just the right amount of humor to offset his tragic past."
—*RT Book Reviews* on
Beauty and the Reclusive Prince

"A warm and engaging story about two people
without family starting a new one of their own."
—*RT Book Reviews* on *Bride by Royal Appointment*

Praise for Nina Harrington

"I look forward to reading this author's next release…and her next…
and her next. It truly is a stunning debut with characters that will
remain in your thoughts long after you have closed the book."
—*pinkheartsocietyreviews.blogspot.com* on *Always the Bridesmaid*

"Rich with emotion, and pairing two truly special characters,
this beautiful story is simply unforgettable. A keeper."
—*RT Book Reviews* on *Hired: Sassy Assistant*

RAYE MORGAN
NINA HARRINGTON

Royal Wedding Bells

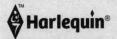

TORONTO NEW YORK LONDON
AMSTERDAM PARIS SYDNEY HAMBURG
STOCKHOLM ATHENS TOKYO MILAN MADRID
PRAGUE WARSAW BUDAPEST AUCKLAND

ISBN-13: 978-0-373-17752-3

ROYAL WEDDING BELLS

First North American Publication 2011

Copyright © 2011 by Harlequin Books S.A.

The publisher acknowledges the copyright
holders of the individual works as follows:

THE PRINCE'S FORBIDDEN LOVE
Copyright © 2011 by Helen Conrad

THE ORDINARY KING
Copyright © 2011 by Nina Harrington

Recycling programs
for this product may
not exist in your area.

www.Harlequin.com

Printed in U.S.A.

RAYE MORGAN
The Prince's Forbidden Love

Dear Reader,

One of the hardest things a parent has to learn is when to let go. You spend years protecting and coaxing and urging—and then you have to learn to stand back and let the youngster try his wings on his own and sail out into life—or crash into the rocks, which happens, too. How can you know when he or she is old enough, strong enough? How can you recognize that magic moment when the adult waiting inside begins to shine through and you have to step back and let it happen?

Think how it must be even harder for a guardian to release a ward, especially one he's truly cared for. There is sometimes a special tug between adored child and something else that is developing—something bigger, more profound. And if the guardian has found himself drifting into a fascination that threatens to capture his heart, how difficult to hold back, to do the responsible thing and let the ward find her own footing rather than trying to manipulate her into being the one and only one.

That is the dilemma dealt with in *The Prince's Forbidden Love*. Hope you enjoy wrestling with that theme.

Happy reading!

Raye Morgan

CHAPTER ONE

Crown Prince Andre Rastava of the Royal House of Diamante, rulers of Gemania, was bored, and when he got bored he tended to get restless. The noise of the crowd in the casino was giving him a headache, and he found himself shrugging away the caresses of the exotic lady who had draped herself up against his body like a sleazy silk scarf.

What was her name again? It didn't really matter. Lately the women had become as interchangeable as all the other decorative items in his life. He couldn't tell one from another.

"Your Highness?" the croupier nudged, waiting for his call.

He glanced back at the roulette wheel and shrugged, pulling his tie loose and shoving back the sleeves of his Italian suit.

"Let it ride," he said, his voice hoarse. It hardly mattered if he won or lost. He wasn't really here for the gambling. Though few around him realized it, he had a far more dangerous game to play. That usually kept his attention razor-sharp.

But for some reason not tonight. Maybe it was the early spring heat wave coming in on the winds through the high mountain pass and numbing his senses. Or maybe it was the throbbing pain from the shrapnel that still lodged in his leg from the near miss he'd had in the explosion of his car the previous year. Or maybe he was just getting tired of this lifestyle.

He looked at the snifter of cognac that no one ever seemed to notice he seldom touched. It was all part of the show—just like the two young ladies who were his guests here this evening, just like the gaming, just like the setting. Just like the onlookers who didn't know they were merely part of the audience to this play.

He looked out at them, at all the interested faces. Many of the men gazed at him with awe and a bit of envy. The women tended to smile as though hoping to catch his attention, even if for a fleeting moment. They seemed like nice enough people. Why were they watching him? For just a second he felt almost apologetic.

It's all an act, people, he wanted to say. *Don't you get it?*

But something happened that stopped that thought cold. As his gaze skittered through the crowd it met a pair of dark brown eyes that took his breath away. He knew those eyes. He knew that pretty, comical face with its sprinkling of freckles over the pert nose and its impatient pout.

But…it couldn't be.

Shaking his head, as though to clear it of a fantasy, he closed his eyes and tried to erase her. But when he looked again she was still there, her blond curls like an enchanted cloud around her pretty face, her dark eyes blazing accusingly.

One sleek eyebrow rose as he stared back, curling his lip. He was letting her know from the start that he regretted nothing. She could take her complaints elsewhere. At least that was what he'd hoped to convey. But something in those soft dark eyes held him a beat too long. And suddenly he found himself sinking into her gaze in a way that caught at his breathing. Strange. He pulled away and blinked quickly. This wasn't like him.

His number won again. A larger crowd was gathering, which didn't help under the best of circumstances. His wide mouth twisted as he frowned and glanced at the croupier. The young man shrugged imperceptibly and appeared a bit bewildered. Prince Andre motioned to have his winnings collected and prepared to leave, ignoring the murmurings of the crowd and the entreaties of his two young female companions.

But when he rose and turned toward where he'd seen her she was gone.

Had he been dreaming? He scanned the room. No, he was still living in the real world. There she was, walking quickly toward the outer terrace that overlooked the lake, her honey-blond hair bouncing against her lovely back, the skirt of her yellow sundress swishing about her shapely knees.

He hesitated for another second or two. Was he sure it was Julienne? How could it be? His ward should be living under veritable lock and key in the mountain convent where she'd been ensconced for years now. The entire staff was under strict orders not to let her roam free. Was this merely a lookalike? A twin sister he'd never known about?

No matter. In any case, he had to check it out. He turned to leave the roulette table.

"Your Highness," the exotic beauty was saying, reaching for him. "Please…."

"May we go with you?" her Scandinavian partner was asking plaintively. "We're supposed to accompany you to—"

"Find Rolfo," he said shortly, barely glancing at them.

"He will see that you are taken care of. I have something urgent I must attend to."

And he was off.

Princess Julienne was hurrying toward an exit, if only she could find one. She'd come up in an elevator, but now she was disoriented and wasn't sure where it was. This had been a bad idea. She should have known better.

This entire scene was alien to her. She'd never been in a casino before. She hadn't really been in a city before— at least, not for years. She was a convent girl. What had made her think she could come here and beard the lion in his den? She'd thought she would have the element of surprise, but she hadn't realized he would have every other advantage.

He was so darn scary. Funny how she'd forgotten about that. Strength, power, and a casual disregard for danger seemed to exude from him like she'd never seen in anyone else. There was no way she could fight him. What had she been thinking? She wasn't going to talk him into anything. She'd do better making a run for it.

A little part of her had hoped. She hadn't remembered him as an ogre, exactly, and she'd thought she might be able to spark a little tiny flare of compassion in him. If she just had a chance to talk to him, face to face, surely....

But, no. She'd seen now how the land lay. There had been a time when she'd thought he cared about her, that he wanted her to be happy as well as useful to the crown. He was out of her life as far as she was concerned. He could just stay here with his fancy ladies and gamble and—

She stopped herself, biting her tongue as her gaze darted about, searching for a way back to the parking lot.

She'd left Popov, the driver from the convent, down below with the car. Dear, sweet Popov. He was the only person she could trust. Now…could she trust him to take her to the border and help her get across? Once she told him that was what she wanted, would he still be her only friend? Or would he become just as mean as everyone else?

She made one last attempt to find an elevator, but she'd lost track of where she'd come out on the floor, and besides, she was out on a wide terrace now. There were so many people, so much noise and color, with the blue waters of the lake shimmering behind it all. But ahead she saw an opening to wide, curving steps and she hurried forward, hoping to take them down.

The question remained—was he following her?

She glanced back over her shoulder as she started down the huge sweeping staircase to street level. There was some sort of commotion back on the casino floor. That only spurred her on, and she raced down the steps, leaping from one to the next, her heart in her throat. Her only hope was to make it back to the parking area and find her driver before anyone could catch her.

She was going to get away.

Prince Andre was finding it necessary to push himself through a growing knot of people who were gathering about the table, as though just watching him play would make them rich. He cleared them just as she disappeared down the stairs, and by the time he got to the railing he could see that she was more than halfway down to the street. If she reached it before he caught her she would melt into the tourist traffic and be gone for good. He hesitated for barely a second. His impulse was to call out to her, but something told him she wouldn't obey his commands and he might as well save himself the trouble.

He glanced at the wrought-iron decorative work that led from one window to another on the outer building walls.

The thought of his bad leg only deterred him for half a second, and then he was up on the railing and reaching for the ironwork. A shift in balance, a lunge for a hand-hold, a leap of faith, and he landed, upright and poised, right in front of Julienne as she made it to the last step.

That brought her up short and caught her attention, and she stared at him, her eyes wide as saucers.

"Wow," she said, thoroughly impressed.

The small crowd lining the upper railing sighed in awe as well, and a couple of them even clapped.

He managed to cover up the gasp of pain his leg gave him upon landing and glared at her.

"So it *is* you."

She nodded, still thunderstruck by his Tarzan stunt. Funny, but that pretty much fit in with the way she'd always seen him—a bit larger than life. And it did appeal to her feminine senses.

But then, he always had. She gazed at him almost hungrily, taking in all of him. It had been so long since she'd last seen him. She realized he considered her nothing but a hindrance, a ward who had been thrust upon him, a responsibility he didn't need. But she'd always thought of him as her own personal hero. Only lately he hadn't been living up to that part.

"What the hell are you doing here?" he demanded, looking fierce.

She frowned at him, lifting her chin defiantly. She wasn't a child any longer and she wasn't going to let him treat her like one. "Don't swear at me. I'm your ward. You're supposed to be a role model for me."

"And you're supposed to be at the convent, preparing for your wedding."

She made a face and looked guilty, her gaze sliding to the side. "Yes, about that..."

He groaned. Trouble. Nothing but trouble. He could see it in her eyes.

A crowd was forming on the street level as well now. Before he knew it the paparazzi would get wind of this, and then there would be hell to pay. It was time to disappear from view.

"Come along," he told her gruffly, taking her hand and beginning to lead her toward a shadowy space behind the stairs. "We need to talk."

"Exactly what I was thinking," she said pluckily, though the sense of his forceful personality was wafting over her like a tidal wave and she knew she had to resist. "We've got a lot of catching up to do."

That wasn't quite what he had in mind, but he didn't comment. Instead, he led her in through an unmarked door and then onto a private elevator that opened to his coded entry. Soon they were hurtling toward the penthouse of the ten-story building, and Prince Andre's suite.

He looked her over, glancing sideways. She'd always been pretty, but she'd developed a luminous quality since he'd last seen her—a sort of inner glow that reminded him of angels.

Angels! He gritted his teeth. Just as he'd feared, she was more appealing than ever. He had to get her back to the convent as quickly as possible. Once she was married to his cousin, Prince Alphonso, he could wash his hands of her.

The elevator doors opened right into the Prince's suite, making Julienne blink with surprise. As she stepped out she looked about, eyes wide with wonder. Everything was shiny chrome, gleaming dark cherry wood and smoky tinted glass, with sleek leather couches and huge abstract art pieces on the walls. One side of the room was a floor-to-ceiling picture window, overlooking the lake and showing off the snow-capped mountaintops in the distance.

When she'd been eight years old she'd gone on a trip to Paris with her parents and she'd stayed in places almost as elegant as this. But it had been a long time since then, and she'd become used to the simple, rough-hewn décor of the convent. This place took her breath away.

"Nice," she said casually, trying hard not to come across as the wide-eyed-in-wonder country bumpkin she felt like.

"I like it," he replied shortly. "Why don't you sit down?" he added, nodding toward one of the softer-looking couches. "I'll get you a drink."

"A drink?" she said hopefully.

"Nothing fancy," he warned her. "I think I've got some lemonade in the refrigerator."

"Oh," she said, somewhat deflated.

She'd been hoping he would serve an adult beverage, as though it were her due—a sort of sign that he understood she was of age now. No such luck. He still thought she merited lemonade. She was used to wine of a sort with meals at the convent, but it was hardly more than colored water as far as she'd ever been able to ascertain. His lemonade would probably provide more punch, even if it didn't contain a bit of alcohol.

He watched the expressions change on her face and felt as though he could read every thought that was coursing through her mind. He had to turn away to hide his grin. Despite being fundamentally annoyed that she'd popped up into his world like this without warning, he couldn't help but be charmed by her—as he always was.

What the heck—he supposed he could give her some vodka in her lemonade to make her feel as though she were doing something slightly sophisticated.

"Here you go," he said, handing her a tall frosted glass.

"I added a little something, but just barely enough for you to feel it. We can't have you going back to the convent tipsy."

She smiled at him, delighted, but at the same time vowing that the convent was the last place for her tonight.

He dropped smoothly onto the arm of the couch and looked down at her. He knew he should call Mother Superior to let her know Julienne was with him, but he didn't want to. Surely they would try to contact him when they realized she was gone. And then he would have to make plans as to when he would take her back. Much as he wanted her back where she belonged, he began to realize that she wouldn't have come if there wasn't a serious problem. The goal was to get her to the church on time, with as little hassle as possible.

Still, he would have to take it easy and figure out the best way to accomplish that. Barking orders wouldn't get her to do what he wanted. Cooperation was his goal. In order to achieve that he had to find out what had motivated her into coming to find him this way.

He grimaced. Being sensitive to the needs of others wasn't usually uppermost in his mind. He was used to being catered to. Time for him to learn to stretch himself a little.

"Okay, Julienne," he began slowly, feeling his way. "Explain to me just exactly what you're doing here."

His voice was low, but with enough command to let her know he expected a complete and coherent answer.

She took a sip, nodded approvingly, and smiled up at him again, waving one hand with a flourish.

"This is merely a courtesy call," she told him cheekily. "I thought, as my guardian, you might like to know what I plan to do with my life."

He frowned, wary, but still in control of his reactions.

"As your guardian, I already know what you're going to do with your life. In fact, I planned it myself. No need for you to bother."

"Ah, but that's where you've gone wrong." She took another sip, just for bravery, and set the drink down on the glass coffee table. "You see, I'm no longer a minor, no longer in a position to be your ward." She took a deep breath and faced him squarely, her gaze simple and direct. "In fact, I quit. I'm old enough to be on my own. And that is what I choose to do."

He looked pained. "Julienne, you know very well your life was mapped out seven years ago as part of the Treaty of Salvais."

She glanced down at the drink, began to reach for it, then drew her hand back and nodded quickly. "I know. I know. But, you see, that was done without my consent, and—"

"Your consent!" He shook his head, losing control of his patience a bit. "Julienne, your wedding is in less than a week. You can't back out now. The invitations are out. The gifts are streaming in. It's too late to stop the momentum. It's going to happen, whether you like it or not."

She didn't look convinced. In fact, she looked downright resentful.

"And are you planning to show up this time?" she asked, challenging him with her dark, honest gaze. "Or do you have your usual 'business to attend to' instead?"

His head went back in reaction. She'd pushed exactly the button that was guaranteed to open the floodgates to the guilt he felt about his guardianship. Over the last few years he'd avoided seeing her, missing every Christmas, every birthday. He knew his actions had hurt her. But it couldn't be helped. As her guardian, he had to protect her from predatory men. What he'd never expected when he took on that role was that he would be his own prime target.

"Julienne, all this is beside the point. You are required by treaty to marry Prince Alphonso next week, and marry him you will."

She shook her head, lower lip thrust out rebelliously. "I never signed any treaty," she insisted. "I never gave consent."

He jerked to his feet and began to pace the floor, holding back his quick surge of exasperation. Was he going to be forced to go over the whole history with her once again? No, she was just being stubborn. She knew all about the fighting between the three royal houses that had ripped their country apart for generations.

Right now an uneasy truce prevailed, but it had only come about after a long, bloody war. Too many people had died. He thought, with a quick slice of pain, of his own mother, killed by an assassin's bullet. The factions had fought each other to a standstill, and then it had taken a long, torturous struggle of negotiation to finally settle things, and that had only happened once Julienne's parents, the King and Queen of the House of Emeraude, had agreed that she would marry Prince Alphonso when she reached twenty-one years. Their marriage would tie the houses of Emeraude and Diamante together for evermore, and help balance the struggle of power between the three houses.

It had to happen. If she didn't follow through with the treaty's promise, the country was very likely to go up in flames again. No one wanted that, and as one of the architects of the plan he couldn't let it happen. In fact, it was up to him to make sure she followed through.

"Your parents gave all the consent that was needed," he

told her coolly. "The deal was sealed. There is no going back on our word."

"I know all that," she was saying, looking at him earnestly. "But I've thought it over and I think I can fight it in court."

"In court?" He stopped pacing and stared at her, not knowing whether to laugh or cry. Didn't she realize that as far as this went he was pretty much all the "court" she was going to have at her disposal? How could he explain to her? She really didn't have a choice.

"Yes," she said emphatically. "I'm sure forcing me to marry is against my civil rights."

"Really?" he said, still staring at her. "You think you have civil rights?"

She sat up straighter, looking shocked that he would even question that. "Of course. Everyone does. And making me marry someone just to hold a country together doesn't make a lot of sense. I bet there's not another girl in the world who is being expected to do that."

Poor Julienne. He regarded her with a mixture of exasperation and a certain sad bemusement. How had she managed to make it this far without learning that being royal meant you weren't like everyone else? That had its obvious advantages, but there was also a downside. She was stuck. She could twist and turn and try to think of every sort of angle, but there was no escape. She would feel a whole lot better about things once she accepted that and got on with her life. In a strange, convoluted way, her plight touched his heart. But there was nothing he could do to remedy it.

She looked so young, so innocent. The late-afternoon light shafting in through the huge picture window seemed to turn her skin a creamy gold.

"You're probably right," he told her, fighting off the

impulse to reach out and cup her lovely flushed cheek in the palm of his hand. "You're the only one."

He saw the hope that flared in her eyes and he hated to douse it, but it had to be done. He knew it was asking a lot to rest all the culture and peace of one country on the shoulders of one tiny twenty-one-year-old girl. But what was right and what was fair just plain didn't matter. That was the way it was. Her situation was her situation, and if she didn't abide by the rules he'd set up a lot of people might die. It had happened before. It could happen again. They couldn't risk it.

"You're looking at this all wrong," he told her helpfully. "You should be proud of the sacrifice you are making for your country."

Her eyes clouded and she wrinkled her nose. "Sorry. Ask someone else, please."

Was she going to cry? He tensed. If she started to cry it would be impossible to keep his distance and he knew it. But she looked up and smiled at him tremulously. And that was almost as bad.

He had to turn away and begin pacing again. When she sat there looking so adorable, everything in him seemed to yearn toward her. And so he paced, gritting his teeth and searching for strength.

He thought of the first time he'd seen her, when she was only fourteen years old. He'd spent a hard few days negotiating with her parents, the King and Queen, in order to convince them that the only way peace would be achieved would be for them to lock their daughter into a marriage contract that would cement the ties and keep the jealousies in check. With Emeraude and Diamante joined as one, the renegade House of Rubiat wouldn't dare try another power-grab.

They'd invited him to share their dinner, and, though he

usually didn't like to socialize with negotiating partners, he'd liked the two of them well enough, and respected them enough, to make an impulse decision to eat with them. They'd been talking pleasantly when Julienne had come into the room.

"And here she is," her father had said fondly. "The center of all our conversation these days." He'd smiled at his daughter. "Prince Andre, may I present Princess Julienne?"

He remembered rising and giving her a deep bow, while she curtsied in her charming way. He recalled smiling at her and thinking she was the cutest thing he'd seen in ages. For just a moment he'd wished he had a young sister about her age, someone he could take under his wing and mentor in the ways of royal life. And that was odd, because he'd never had a thought like that before in his life—nor had he since—and yet that was pretty much what very soon came to pass.

She'd charmed him right from the beginning. She was such a sweet, lively girl, but with a spark of humor and a quick understanding that seemed to belie her young age. He'd liked her immediately.

Only weeks later her parents had been killed when their light plane went down in the mountains. Andre became her guardian from the first, with the consent of all concerned. He'd been the architect of the treaty and it was up to him to make sure its elements were complied with.

He'd brought her to Diamante Castle and treated her like one of the family from the first. King Harold, his father, was busy with affairs of state, his life's work, which he'd thrown himself into with a vengeance once Nadine, his wife, queen and Andre's mother, had been killed by a sniper years before. They rarely conferred. Harold was the sort of man who seemed weighed down by his work.

To the casual observer, he was an old grouch. But not to Andre. Andre knew the tragic sorrow he carried with him at all times and he loved him for it.

Still, his father never showed much interest in the young, lively and engagingly coltish girl who'd come to live with them, and it was up to Andre, despite the fact that they were less than ten years apart in age, to act the part of elder authority along with everything else. And the two of them had got on well together. He looked back on those days as some of the happiest of his life.

As she'd grown older, he'd known it couldn't last. And then came her eighteenth birthday and the dance—and the kiss.

That was when he knew he had to call upon some inner well of strength to get through the next few years until she married. And here they were, with six days left. Was he going to make it?

CHAPTER TWO

"ALL right, Julienne," Prince Andre said, sitting down on the couch again. "Come clean. How did you manage to escape from the convent?"

She bit her lip and gazed at him levelly. "You see, just the concept of my having to 'escape' is offensive. I'm a grown woman."

He hardly knew how to counter that, because she was right. But that didn't matter, so he ignored it.

"You must have had help."

She hesitated, then nodded. "There's a person who's always available to help me. He drove me down."

He felt a flash of anger, but he stifled it. He looked at her, his gaze veiled. "I see. Is he waiting for you outside?"

She hesitated. "I'm afraid he is. Should I…?"

Andre felt every muscle tense. "Does he have a mobile?"

She shook her head. "We don't have cell phones at the convent."

A twenty-one year old woman without a phone. How was that possible?

"Where is he?" he asked crisply. "I'll have someone tell him to go back. I'll handle your travels from here on out."

She hesitated, feeling a bit deflated. "But…"

He turned and pinned her with a penetrating look. Her

reluctance to do as he asked made him suspicious. "Is he your boyfriend?"

"Oh!" She laughed at the concept. He was old enough to be her grandfather. "No, not at all. He's an old man."

Andre frowned. "Older than I am?"

"You?" She looked shocked at the concept. "You're not old."

He grinned. He couldn't help it. "Oh, Julienne, you have no idea." His gaze met hers and held for a beat too long, and then they both looked quickly away.

"And anyway," she said, reaching for her lemonade, "where in the world would I get a boyfriend?"

Yes, that had been the whole justification for sending her to be educated in the convent. Hopefully she was telling the truth, and things had worked out just as he'd planned. Lots of study, lots of peace and spirituality, and a complete lack of male companionship. Perfect. The only trouble was, she seemed to have picked up some bad ideas anyway.

Julienne looked around the room nervously, wondering how she was going to cope with this questioning. So far so good—but she was used to the convent, used to quiet. She prayed and read and recited poetry and bible verses. And she dreamed.

For the last few years she'd helped the sisters with the younger girls. She'd been old enough to go away to university, but when she wrote to her guardian about applying he didn't respond.

So she stayed at the convent and lived a simple, quiet life. Mother Superior had allowed her to enroll in some online college courses and helped her study—and in fact she was well on her way to earning a degree in European history. But lately her interest had flagged. History wasn't really where her heart lay. It lay in a very secret place where she'd been forbidden to go—many times. What she lived for was not allowed to someone of her stature. The fact was, the Princess of Emeraude loved…to cook.

Pastries, mostly. Fortunately the woman who was the convent cook—and Popov's wife—thought her ambitions were wonderful and indulged her whenever she could get away with it.

But that was then. Now she was in the real world, dealing with a real man, and she knew she had to be on her toes. And she definitely did not want him to know about the pastry business. That was her special secret.

"Okay," he said, still not clear on what her day had been like before she'd walked into the casino. "So you found someone to drive you down here to the city. But you didn't tell them at the convent that you were leaving?"

"Oh, no. They would never have let me go."

He nodded, feeling slightly reassured.

"In fact," she went on, feeling chatty now, "I put a 'do not disturb' sign on my door, saying that I was studying for an exam. Then I rigged up a dummy in my bed and tiptoed out."

He groaned and looked pained. "That is the oldest trick in the book."

She nodded. "It's old because it works. I've done it before."

"What?" He was back to visions of dangerous boyfriends and hot cars, despite what she'd said, and it was shocking how much he hated that scene as he imagined it. "Julienne…"

She shook her head at him. "Don't worry, it was just so that I could take walks in the hills without people hunting me down and telling me to be careful every step I took. The convent is a nice, quiet place, but everyone knows what you're doing at every minute of the day and it can get suffocating."

"Oh." It was embarrassing how relieved he felt. "I see."

"So when I decided I had to come find you, I used it again. It was easy."

He grimaced. "Why did you feel you had to come all this way? Why not write a letter or send an email? Or even pick up the phone and give me a call?"

She looked outraged by his suggestions. "Are you kidding? I wrote letter after letter detailing all the indignities I was forced to live under at the convent."

He was glad he'd missed those. "Itemizing your complaints, you mean?" he noted cynically.

"Of course. And I've got a few."

He grimaced. "Spare me."

"Why should I? You haven't exactly been a hands-on guardian of late. I thought I deserved a little more personal care. But you never responded." She shrugged. "If the mountain won't come to you, you've got to go to the mountain."

He raised a cynical eyebrow. "I'm a mountain now, am I?"

She favored him with an impish grin. "Kind of. You're big and scary, anyway."

He groaned, but she ignored that and went on.

"I begged you to come and see what conditions were like for yourself. Letter after letter. Didn't you read any of them?"

He shrugged. "In truth, I don't remember reading anything of the kind." He frowned, thinking that over. "Perhaps my secretary read them." He looked up and decided to go a step further. "Read them and thought them too childish to pass on to me."

"Oh!" Now she was angry. "That's just outrageous."

He bit back his grin and pretended to agree. "You're absolutely right. She should have let me know how things stood."

"Indeed," Julienne said indignantly, ready to confront the woman on the spot. "Where is she?" she added, looking around as though she thought she might be lurking in the shadows.

Andre forced back the smile that threatened. "I'll let her know you were asking after her."

"You do that," she said, looking at him suspiciously. "I think she should be reprimanded."

He shook his head. "Sorry, can't do that. She's not working for me any longer. In fact, she recently left on a round-the-world cruise." His mouth tilted at the corners as he prepared to give her the whole story. "She married an itinerant poker player she met in the casino. They plan to spend their lives aboard cruise ships, traveling from one port to the next."

She stared at him for a moment, then made a face. "That sounds crazy."

And he agreed. "Oh, it is."

She looked at him speculatively, blinking a time or two. "But lovely at the same time. Traveling from place to place." She sighed. "I've never really travelled at all."

Ah, here was his opening, and he took it with vigor. Dropping down beside her on the couch, he leaned in.

"Once you marry Alphonso you can do as you please. Travel. Shop. Eat at fancy restaurants. No more convent. You'll have your own palace. The world will be your oyster."

She stared into his eyes for a long moment, then shook her head slowly. "No, it won't," she said perceptively. "He'll be in charge. I'll have to do what he says. It will be worse than the convent." She made a face and threw up her hands. "You see, that's just my point. The whole world gets to go off and do crazy things except for me. I don't get to do even normal things."

He sighed. It was becoming clear that this was going to take lnger than he'd thought. He glanced at his watch.

"How about this?" he suggested. "We'll go down and get something to eat, talk for a while longer, and then I'll drive you back to the convent. Sound good?"

She stared at him. He just refused to get it, didn't he? She wasn't going back to the convent.

His telephone rang and he excused himself, disappearing into what she assumed must be the bedroom to answer it. She sat stiffly where she was and stared out the huge glass window. It was so disappointing. She'd been so sure—once she saw him again, once they'd had a chance to talk and she'd let him know how she felt—that he would see things her way and even understand why she couldn't do this.

She should have followed her first instincts and just made a run for the border. Now she wouldn't have as good a head start. But she would go. She had no choice, really. It was that or consign herself to a life of misery.

Why couldn't he see her point of view? She'd once thought they had a special rapport, a unique connection that held them together as friends forever. Now she wasn't so sure. He didn't want to hear her side. There was really no hope. So why was she hanging around, waiting to be driven back to the convent? She had to get out of here while she had the chance.

She glanced at the bedroom door. From the sound of it, he was still talking on the phone. Rising from the couch, she walked quickly toward the elevator she'd come up in. All she needed was a little time. She might be able to make the border yet.

* * *

Andre came out of the bedroom frowning, not pleased with the news he'd just received, but all that flew out the window as he looked around the room and realized Julienne was gone.

Well, that had been stupid. He should have known she would be a flight risk. He only hoped it wasn't too late to stop her.

The elevator had a kill switch and he used it now, then headed for the stairs. If she was still on her way down he would catch her at the bottom. If she'd already left the building he would be lucky to find her again. Ever.

Julienne had just reached the ground floor when she heard the gears grinding to a halt.

"Oh, no," she whispered in despair. She knew what that meant. He'd caught her again. She tried punching the door button but nothing moved, and she sighed, waiting for the inevitable.

It seemed forever until the doors slid noiselessly open and Andre stood waiting, his arms crossed over his chest and a dark look on his face.

"Gotcha," was all he said.

She was chilled by the frosty look in his blue eyes, like caverns of ice, but she glared at him anyway. She expected him to join her on the elevator, but instead he reached in and took her hand and pulled her out onto the tiled pavement.

"You want to show me where your boyfriend is?" he said coldly. "I'm sure he's out here somewhere close."

"He's not my—!" She stopped herself and heaved a sigh as she rolled her eyes. She wasn't going to give him the satisfaction of answering. Raising her chin, she looked away.

"Come on," he encouraged, sweeping his arm out

toward the street and the multi-level parking structure across the way. "Where is he?"

Folding her arms across her chest, she looked resolutely in the other direction. "I have no idea," she said evenly.

He waited a moment, studying her profile and hoping for more information. When she didn't say anything more, he shrugged.

"Okay," he said shortly. "If you won't talk, we might as well go eat. Come on." He tucked her hand into the crook of his arm and began to escort her out into the lower level of the casino. She tried to pull her hand away at first, but he wasn't letting it go and she decided it was just too embarrassing to start a tug-of-war. Besides, she had to admit she sort of liked the way it felt, letting him escort her this way.

He liked it, too. He only hoped no one recognized her or did a quick internet search to figure out who she was. If so, the media would know next. He glanced around at the hungry female stares following their progress through the crowd, and he winced. Sometimes it seemed as though every woman he met was measuring him for a groom's coat with her eyes. And why not? After all, he'd been considered the most eligible bachelor in the country for the last ten years. But he'd learned to guard himself from relationships of any kind.

The one close female friend he'd had was his cousin Giselle, but that had pretty much ended when she'd turned her back on royalty and thrown her lot in with the common man. That was something he could never do. He was born and bred to royalty, and when his father died he would be king. It was nothing less than his place in the world.

That was what Julienne had to learn. She had her place, too, and it would make her life much easier if she would accept it. Looking at her, he could see she was enjoying the attention. Hopefully, this would begin a reassessment on her part.

As they walked through the crowd and into the restaurant Julienne noticed the ripple of interest Andre evoked everywhere they went. Despite her anger with him, and the circumstances, she couldn't help but feel a frisson of excitement herself. He was so handsome, and it felt so good to have his arm and…

"Oh!" she said, suddenly realizing she was wearing a simple cotton sundress and every other woman in sight was dressed to the nines. She grabbed Andre's arm with her other hand and leaned close.

"I'm not dressed for dinner," she whispered, casting a worried glance at the *maître d'*.

He covered her hand with his own and looked down at her. A wave of tenderness came over him, and at the same time there was a strange feeling in his chest.

"Don't worry," he told her softly. "We're eating in a private room."

"Oh."

She seemed relieved, but still nervous, and yet he noted she had enough of the royal instinct to walk through the main dining room with her head held high and proud.

He opened the door to let her in to the private space, then closed it again and pulled her close for a moment.

"You could be naked," he said softly, touching her hair, "and there would still be no doubt that you are a princess." He smiled at her. "Bravo."

She was breathless. Though he released her quickly, and turned to pull out a chair for her, the intimacy of his touch and his words left a tingle in her blood. If only…

She wouldn't let herself think that thought through. He

was her guardian, not her lover. She had to be satisfied with what she could get. Or try to, at any rate.

Andre ordered for them both—grilled salmon with a saffron curry puree, cous-cous, and a mint-green apple salad. Every bite was so delicious it was difficult to remember that they were enemies now.

But he managed to remind her.

"You see, Julienne," he told her between courses, "being royal gives you access to private rooms, exquisite meals, the best wines. Why would you want to throw that away?"

She took a sip of the wine. The only relationship it could possibly have to the liquid they poured in her glass at the convent was the rich golden color. But she wasn't going to admit that to him at this point. Instead, she turned and gave him a gimlet eye.

"I've lived twenty-one years with this little invisible paste crown on my head," she told him tartly. "It's like being in prison—and being innocent of whatever crime landed you there in the first place." She shrugged. "It's the age-old lament. I just gotta be free."

He shook his head and she knew he thought she was whining.

"You have probably been the most protected young lady on the face of the earth," he pointed out.

"I'd rather be free than protected," she told him in no uncertain terms.

He shook his head again, looking her over with a bemused smile. "You don't know what you're talking about."

Her royal chin rose again. "I think I have a bit of an inkling," she told him firmly. "I've stared matrimony in the face and I've decided it's not for me." Her glance his way was cool and flippant. "And I'll bet that's more than you've ever done. You haven't come close, have you?"

To her surprise, something flashed in his clear blue

eyes—something that signaled pain and an emotion she wasn't sure she recognized. Her words had wounded him in some way.

"You shouldn't make bets on things you don't understand," he said calmly, reaching for his wine.

She blinked and didn't answer back. She'd brought up something that had upset him and she wished she hadn't.

She had assumed he was a playboy and that was what he had always been. Was there something else? Had someone broken his heart in the past? She swallowed hard and looked down at her plate, wishing she could learn to keep quiet when on unfamiliar ground. To think she'd hurt him was like a knife in her chest, but she couldn't think of a thing she could do to undo it.

The waiter brought dessert—a gorgeous creation of three types of chocolate intertwined and topped off with a heavenly puff of whipped cream. Andre wasn't hungry any longer, and he set it aside after two small bites, but Julienne devoured the entire thing, commenting on flavors and techniques as though she were an expert in this sort of thing.

He sat back, entertained by her commentary, entertained by her obvious relish of the sweet, and generally enjoying watching her, unable to stop. He liked the look of her so much he was like an addict. He couldn't stay away. Everything about her was fresh and free and beautiful. He felt faded and old hat. She was new. He didn't want to sully what she was. She was too special.

Still, he couldn't sit here watching her forever. They both knew very well that she shouldn't have come down to find him in the first place, but now that she was here he supposed he was going to have to do something with her.

But what?

He'd already realized he was not going to be taking her

back to the convent tonight. He needed space and time to work on her reluctance to marry Alphonso. She had to come to an understanding of what her responsibilities were and why she had no choice but to fulfill them. If only he could think of a good way to do it.

Lecturing was doing no good at all. Bullying wouldn't make any more headway. It would just put her back up and make her more defiant.

Bottom line: she had to go back and she had to marry Alphonso. His job would be to convince her of that without real blood being spilled.

But how?

A few different scenarios flitted through his mind and he rejected them in turn. He glanced across the table at where she was sitting, looking like a teenager, with her bargain basement clothes and her legs stuck out in front of her. As he studied her, he wondered what it was about her that appealed to him so strongly—and made her so dangerous. She was certainly pretty, but so were most of the women he knew.

She caught at his emotions rather in the way a passionate aria could transport him into feelings he didn't know he had. She did something mysterious and magical to his soul. And that was why he had to get away from her as soon as possible.

But first he would deal with her concerns and convince her that being a princess was better than the alternative. What could he do to make it appeal to her more?

One thought that came to mind was introducing her to city night-life and what it was like to cruise the clubs as royalty. In one night he could show her what it was like to be a star. After all, she had never been out in public, and had no idea what a princess was actually treated like in her own country. Once she had a bite of the apple…

Might that change her mind? He looked at her sweet face and mentally shook his head. No, that wouldn't really work. Something told him that swelling around the nightclubs with a bunch of substance-impaired groupies lurching after her wasn't going to do the trick, no matter how much her subjects would adore her.

And they *would* fall in love with her at first sight, of that he had no doubt. She was imminently lovable. Even a crusty older man like himself was not immune.

At any rate, he didn't want to be the one to open her world to *la dolce vita* with all its glamourous disguises and ugly underbelly. This merry-go-round he'd been on for the last ten years was a sad and poisonous way to live, and he was heartily sick of it himself.

How had he let this happen to his life? He'd once had high hopes of all the good things he would do for his people and his country—how he would bring in industry, improve education, raise the standard of living for all. Somehow he'd become bogged down in trying to keep the alliance together in order to avoid another war, and he spent his days playing this soul-deadening role in order to do his part.

Funny how it had taken the arrival of this fresh, free spirit to show him the truth in that. The times needed to change. But right now he had a mission to accomplish. He had to convince her to marry Alphonso. That was going to take some time. And if she was going to stay with him for a day or two she would obviously need some clothes.

"What size are you?" he asked her.

She looked startled. "Why?"

"I think I'll have my man, Rolfo, pick up some things for you in the hotel shop. He'll bring them up and you can try them on and decide which ones you want to keep."

Her face was transformed. "Clothes?" she whispered,

as though she were receiving a wonderful present, something she could only dream of in the past. "New clothes?"

He couldn't help but laugh at her funny face. If he'd known this was all it took to bring her such joy he'd have been sending her packages from department stores for the last three years.

"We'll see how sophisticated Rolfo's taste is." He pulled out his phone. "I'll get him right on it."

CHAPTER THREE

PRINCE ANDRE escorted Princess Julienne back to his penthouse suite as soon as their meal had run its course. She went willingly enough, though she did have a qualm or two. Had he tempted her with the promise of new clothes just to make sure she didn't try again to make a run for it? Or was she getting a little too suspicious for her own good?

Since her parents had died when she was fourteen, she'd known almost nothing but life in the Diamante Castle—a stark, forbidding structure manned mostly by servants. She'd studied with a governess, and the daughters of local noble families had been brought in to be her friends, but the days when Andre was home were what she'd lived for. Andre was her hero and her best friend. When he showed up, her drab life had suddenly lit up.

But once she'd turned eighteen it had been mostly life in the convent. She was allowed to go back to the castle at Christmas for three days, and for two weeks in the summer she was sent off to stay at the lake house. On her birthday someone would come to visit her bringing presents. Until two years before that someone had been Prince Andre. But without explanation he had stopped coming.

Dear Prince Andre, she mused sarcastically, glancing at him sideways. Her guardian. The man who was in control of her life. And he wouldn't even come to visit her.

They'd told her that he was too busy. They'd said he was an important man and couldn't be bothered. And he hadn't answered her letters.

So she'd finally come to see for herself.

He was busy, all right. Busy living like a playboy. As she thought of it now, she was more furious with him than ever—and that only confirmed her determination to fight him. House of Diamante, House of Emeraude, House of Rubiat—who cared? They could take this royal life, this relic of the past, and they could keep it for themselves. She would have no part of it.

"Did you enjoy the dinner?" he asked her, pulling off his tie and opening his shirt a few more buttons' worth.

She nodded, going back and forth between thinking he was the most handsome man on earth to resenting how he'd treated her over the years.

"It was wonderful," she admitted.

"I'm glad you liked it." His eyes were deep and sultry. "I want you to be happy."

But still he expected her to marry Prince Alphonso.

He left the room and she turned away and looked at the moonlight over the lake. She really didn't know Alphie well, but she'd met him a time or two, and this last summer he'd come to the lake to see her for four days—the longest, dreariest four days of her life.

If only he were more like Andre maybe she could stomach the thought of it. But he wasn't like Andre. Nobody was like Andre. She put her hands against the cool glass and sighed.

He came back into the room, poured himself a drink and got her a lemonade—this time without enhancement. She sat on the long couch and stared at it. He was treating her like a child again, she supposed, but there were so many things she was trying to fight him on, she decided to take a pass on this one.

She was defying him and she was going to go on defying him. What was he going to do about it? Actually, the answer to that terrified her. He was the scariest man she knew. And yet her soul was filled with a pure, crystal-clear, female anger—the anger of a woman who felt she deserved a little more attention than she had been getting. If he thought he was going to start shooting orders at her and having people confined to their quarters and things like that, he could think again. Those tactics weren't going to make her change her mind. This wasn't the old dark ages of the royal world any longer. He couldn't get away with the Anne Boleyn treatment these days. She had a few rights of her own, and he was going to have to listen to her point of view.

She looked down the couch at where he was sitting. He hadn't spoken for a long time and he was staring moodily out the darkened window. Dark curls had fallen over his forehead in a very sexy way. He was so handsome. Her anger began to melt away. She knew he was thinking over the situation and that he was trying to decide what to do with her, how to fix this dilemma. She had a sudden surge of sympathy for him.

"Do you remember how we used to play chess?" she asked him.

He looked up and met her gaze. Reluctantly, he gave her a half-smile. "Certainly."

"And how I used to let you win?" she added mischievously.

"Let me win?" A look of outrage flashed over his face, and then he laughed. It was the first genuine laugh she'd seen from him, and a bubble of happiness burst in her chest. This was the Prince Andre she remembered.

Rising, she moved down and sat very close to him.

"I understand that I'm making waves. I understand that this is a problem that you feel you have to solve. But you know what? You don't really have to solve it."

"No?" He searched her eyes as though looking for a hopeful sign.

"No. I'm sure one of my cousins from my uncle's second marriage would be glad to marry him. And that should fulfill…"

He rose, making a sound of disgust. "Julienne, stop it. Your name is on the treaty. You are the only bride Alphonso will accept. And a marriage between the highest-ranked in our two houses is the only thing the Rubiat will accept. If they don't see that happen, they'll feel justified in attacking again."

"I don't understand. Why do they care that much?"

"Tradition. You can't fight it. It's in their blood."

She shook her head. "But why do they care so much about Alphonso and me? What do we mean to their lives?"

"The two of you are nothing. It's the Houses you represent. The royal families. The myths. And their need for power."

She sat very still, thinking that over, wishing she could pull it apart and find a flaw so that she would attack it properly. But very soon she forgot all about that. She was sitting very close to him, her thigh touching his, and little by little that became the whole focus of her mind, her senses, her emotions. She wanted to turn and touch him with her hand. She wanted to press herself to him. She wanted to taste his mouth, breathe his breath, feel his heartbeat against her skin. Her own heart began to pound so loudly she was sure that he must hear it. Her breathing began to pulse with the beat, faster and faster, and she wanted…she wanted…

He rose, suddenly, and left the room, not saying a word.

She turned beet-red where she sat, sure that she'd driven him away with her relentless need for him. It was embarrassing. But it was such a deep part of her she couldn't really regret it.

She knew she loved him. She always had. The fact that she could never have him was her own private tragedy. Tears welled in her eyes.

And then the elevator dinged and she whirled, watching the doors open. In came an enormous rack full of clothes. Her jaw dropped as she watched it arrive.

"Is this for me?" she asked, stunned.

The older man who was pushing the rack stopped and leaned around to smile at her. "I don't know if you remember me, Princess. I'm Rolfo, Prince Andre's assistant. I want you to call on me if you need anything."

"Oh, thank you," she said, though she couldn't take her eyes off the clothes. She went closer, touching one fabric, then another. "What am I to do with all these? I can't possibly wear them all."

"No." He laughed. "You're to go through them and pick out the ones that appeal to you. Try them on. And then make a few choices."

She looked at him, her eyes wide. This was the most delicious moment she'd had in ages.

"How many am I to take?" she asked breathlessly.

"As many as you like, Your Highness."

She shook her head. "But I don't know…"

Her voice trailed off.

"Take your time, Princess," Rolfo said in his kindly manner. "The answers will come to you."

As she turned to begin sorting through the treasure trove she was overwhelmed. It was really too much. For a moment she couldn't speak. She'd spent most of the last seven years wearing a crisp white blouse with a plaid skirt.

She had no idea where to begin. Reaching out, she touched a white lace blouse, a red velvet skirt, a sky-blue fitted silk sheath, and she sighed.

Rolfo watched her for a moment with a smile, then he left so discreetly she forgot he'd ever been there.

Prince Andre reappeared, raising his eyebrows as he surveyed the scene.

"I see Rolfo has brought you quite a stack of clothes," he said. "Go ahead and have some fun choosing some things to wear for the next few days. I've got a couple more calls to make."

He realized that this was only fair. After all, he should have taken care that she'd gotten suitable clothes long ago. She was a princess. It was way past time to put away her schoolgirl clothes.

From the look on her face, he could see this was something she wasn't used to. But that didn't make sense. Why wasn't she amassing some sort of massive trousseau? She was supposed to be preparing for a wedding. Why wasn't someone making sure she was going to her groom properly attired?

With chagrin, he realized *he* was the one who should have been taking care of making sure that happened. Some guardian he was.

And yet he knew why he'd been neglecting his duties. The more he thought about her, the more he wanted to think about her—and that was something he had to avoid. He'd stayed away for a reason, and it appeared others had not jumped in to take up the slack as he would have hoped. For a few seconds he indulged in a flash of anger toward his aunt, the Duchess of Fersuit, who lived with them at the castle off and on. Why hadn't *she* taken over this task? Just how lonely had Julienne been these last few years? And all because he couldn't trust himself to be near her.

But those days were over. He was going to take over this project and get her married, come hell or high water. And once he got through with her she would understand the sort of life she could lead as a princess, as opposed to what it would be like for her if she chose to turn her back on her destiny.

He watched her look happily through the clothes and only half listened to her chatter as she reacted to each piece, holding one up in front of herself in the mirror, then laughing at the effect. There was no denying it. She was enchanting, and he was tempting fate just having her here.

But that was just how it had to be. He was strong enough to handle it. Not easy, but possible. He'd been through danger before. He grinned suddenly, laughing at himself and his preposterous comparison of this danger to those more immediate and physically damaging incidents, like being shot at by a sniper and having his car blow up in his face. He could handle one little twenty-one-year-old girl—couldn't he?

"Shot through the heart," he muttered to himself, shaking his head.

"I am so in love with all these clothes," she said, holding up one outfit, and then another. Suddenly her smile dimmed as she had a thought. "Do you always do this?" she asked curiously.

He looked up, surprised and not sure what she meant. "Do what?" he asked her.

She took a deep breath. "Do you always have Rolfo run down and buy clothes for your girlfriends?" she asked, her eyes dark and luminous. And then she said something kind of mean, though it came out of the flash of pain she was feeling. "I suppose you probably have him buy them nightgowns."

"My girlfriends don't wear nightgowns," he said without thinking, then regretted it as she turned bright red.

"Oh, Julienne." He started toward her, ready to take her hands in his, then stopped himself. "That was just a joke. I didn't mean it. I couldn't resist when you gave me such a perfect opening."

"Okay," she said, trying hard not to sound a bit shaky.

He shook his head, looking at her with pure affection. "Julienne, you are just too…too…"

"Young? Naive? Silly?"

Actually, he'd been thinking more along the lines of adorable, charming, refreshing, delectable…. And now he had to stop, before he said something he would really wish he hadn't—even in his own head.

"Never mind," she said, waving him away. "Go make your phone calls. I'll be here, having fun."

He hesitated. "You won't make another run for it?" he asked softly.

She flashed him a quick smile. "Not right now. I've got too much to do right here."

He grinned and retreated to the bedroom, though he left the door open so that he could keep an eye on her. And when he came back out ten minutes later he found the mood had changed drastically.

No longer sorting through the rack, she was sitting on the couch, arms folded across her chest.

"What's the matter?" he said, startled by the transformation.

She looked up at him, her gaze cloudy. "I can't take any of these clothes."

"What are you talking about?"

She shrugged—all tragedy, all the time. "For one thing, you're trying to bribe me with them."

He stopped in his tracks, looking outraged. "Bribe you? What are you talking about?"

She looked at him accusingly. "That's what this has all been about, hasn't it? The meal, the dessert, the clothes."

She seemed to have a unique gift of finding the exact wording that would make him the angriest. He had to work hard at keeping his fury at bay. Bribe her, indeed!

"How much of a clothing allowance have I given you over the years?" he asked her carefully.

"Clothing allowance?" She looked blank. "I never saw any clothing allowance. I just took what you had Mathilda, the housekeeper, get for me. She would go on shopping trips and come back with the ugliest clothes you've ever seen."

He stared at her, feeling a well of regret growing in the pit of his stomach. She really did have a point, didn't she? "Julienne," he said softly, "I'm so sorry. I never paid enough attention…."

"No, no, it was fine." She shook her head so hard her hair slapped her cheeks. "I had plenty of clothes. And the few times I really needed something special Mathilda found something for me at the Saturday market. Like for Christmas or my birthday."

That wasn't really good enough. She should have had the best. What kind of a jerk was he, anyway?

"You've been the perfect ward," he said, really angry with himself. "And I've been the worst as a guardian. Why didn't you tell me?"

She shrugged. "Remember those emails I sent you?" she pointed out. "And the letters?"

He shook his head. "You deserve some clothes. I owe you."

She began to put things back on hangers. "No thank you," she said softly.

He watched her, frustrated and annoyed—but mostly at himself, not at her. And he wanted her to take some of the clothes. Actually, he wanted a lot of things, but at least *that* was doable.

"Are you going to wear your sundress to bed?" he asked archly.

She looked up at him and made a face. "No."

"Then you're going to have to take something, aren't you?"

"No," she said stoutly, though she was beginning to see his point.

He was about to make a response, but his mobile rang and he flipped it open impatiently. "Yes?" he said.

She went on putting the clothes away.

"Good," he said to his phone companion. "Okay, I'll tell her."

She stopped, looking at him questioningly as he closed the phone and turned her way.

He looked at her with a faint, hopeful smile. "I take it you understand you're going to have to stay here tonight? But don't worry. In the morning I'll take you back."

She frowned and faced him bravely. "No. I won't go."

His smile faded. "You will go."

She shook her head. He searched her eyes.

"I can read the thoughts whirring in your clever little mind, Julienne. You have plans. But I'm afraid I'm still a step ahead of you."

"Oh?"

"Yes. Rolfo found your driver. I've sent him back to the convent." He was smiling again. "So I'm afraid any run for the border you might have had in mind will have to be postponed."

She looked away, biting her lip. He was right. Without

Popov, her plans were down the drain. Now what was she going to do?

"Sorry about that," he added, and she felt a shiver of outrage at his attitude. He could at least try to understand her point of view. But she had to admit his taunting tone put a different light on things. And now she *was* going to need some clothes, just to survive.

But only a few. Looking back at the rack, she began to pick through all the things she'd loved at first sight, rejecting one after another and reaching for some simpler items—a pair of jeans, a jersey pullover, and of course a basic nightgown. It was time to have a more honest romance with fashion.

Andre showed her the room she could use for the night. It was fairly plain, but the queen-sized bed looked like luxury to a young woman who was used to the thin, firm sleeping arrangements at the convent.

He looked at her thoughtfully as she stowed her new clothes away in a drawer in the bureau.

"We really should have a chaperone," he noted, almost to himself.

She thought he was nuts. "Of course," she responded with a hint of sarcasm. She looked up at him, her eyes wide with mock innocence. "Maybe you can call one of your lady-friends from the casino? I'm sure either one would be happy to come and be my pal for the evening."

He knew she was needling him, but he grinned. "Don't be ridiculous."

"I see. Perfect companions for you, but not for me."

"Exactly."

She shook her head. "Don't you have staff with you?"

"No. I prefer to be alone."

"But…"

"I have Rolfo, my valet, and a couple of bodyguards

available at a moment's notice. But they are very discreet. You won't even know it when you see them." He hesitated over the term *valet*. After all, Rolfo was a lot more than that to him. Still, that wasn't something he could explain to her right now.

"They tell me you spend a lot of time gracing the pages of the tabloids. But, since I'm not allowed to read the papers until they're censored, I don't know that first-hand."

His mouth twisted. What could he say? He was perfectly happy that someone was keeping his lurid image and all the make-believe stories away from her. It was all garbage anyway.

"Let's talk about your wedding," Andre said suddenly.

"It's *your* wedding," she responded crisply, rising and going to the expanse of glass overlooking the lake. The lights of the city were reflected in the inky black water. "You're the one who planned it."

"Most women love to talk about weddings," he said, slightly exasperated. "Why don't you want to talk about yours?"

Turning to face him, she put her hands on her hips. "I'm not having a wedding, Andre. I don't want to marry Alphonso."

"*Prince* Alphonso," he corrected sharply.

"Prince Alphonso," she repeated dutifully. "Or, as I prefer to call him, Prince Dweeb."

He frowned. "Enough of that. He's a perfectly decent and respectable young man."

"That may be, but I don't love him."

"Love?"

He had to bite back his original response. She was still so young. She had no idea how naive she sounded. Love had nothing to do with this. He searched her wide, innocent eyes, wondering how to explain that to her.

"No one is asking you to love him," he said carefully at last. "But you have to marry him. Everyone expects it. The two of you were betrothed years ago. It's too late to change your mind. If you two don't marry, all hell will break loose." He shook his head impatiently. "The wedding will go forward as planned."

He waited for anger, or at least tears. That was the way most of the women of his acquaintance usually fought their battles. But Julienne was gazing at him levelly, as though searching for the chink in his armor, the weak spot she could use in her attack. Walking over to the couch, she flounced down not far from him.

"Just how well do you know Alphonso?" she asked him at last.

He blinked at her, nonplussed. "I know his mother."

"There you go. You don't know him at all, do you?"

"I've seen him. I've met him." He avoided her gaze. Actually, now that he thought about it, he knew where she was coming from. The young man had been no paragon of manliness the last time they'd been together. But he was young. He would grow into his role quickly enough. He turned back and looked at her.

"But, Julienne, that isn't the point. It doesn't matter what Alphonso is like. He's a symbol."

"I'm supposed to be satisfied marrying a symbol?" She threw out both hands. "That's it? That's my life?"

"You think I don't understand what you're going through? Am I not royal?"

"Yes, but you…you…"

"I have to abide by the rules and the responsibilities just like you do."

She shook her head, looking at him rebelliously. "But it seems like you *like* it."

His head jerked back as though she'd slapped him. "No,

Julienne," he said coldly. "I've had to deal with my own disappointments. Being royal gives us some incredible benefits. At the same time it means we aren't allowed to live like others do." He sighed and looked out at the midnight lake. "Sometimes it doesn't seem fair. Sometimes it isn't. But it remains our reality."

She stared at him, wondering what had happened. From the haunted look in his deep blue eyes, she knew something had.

"Tell me," she whispered. She reached out but she couldn't quite touch him. "Tell me what happened to you."

He gave her a scathing look and turned away. "Nothing happened to me."

She didn't believe that, but she could see he wasn't going to tell her anything. "The thing about Alphonso is—"

He rose abruptly. "Enough. I don't need to hear all these complaints about Alphonso. It's your duty to marry him."

Walking to the desk along the far wall, he sank into the chair and pulled out a stack of papers, beginning to sort through them. She watched for a moment, then rose herself and began to stroll around the room, looking at various pieces of art on the bookshelves, and at some of the books stacked there, too.

But, inevitably, she was drawn to the desk where he was working.

"So you're missing a secretary?" she noted, looking over his shoulder at the letter he was reading.

"That I am," he acknowledged, giving her a quick smile.

She bit her lip. A new idea suddenly occurred to her. At first thought it seemed a real winner, though she had a feeling he wasn't going to agree. Still—nothing ventured, nothing gained. She might as well throw it out there and see what his reaction might be.

"Hey, *I* could be your secretary."

He looked up in surprise, then a look of distaste swept over his handsome face. "No, you couldn't."

But the more she thought about it, the more she liked the idea. "Yes. Don't you see? It would be perfect."

He shook his head, dismissing it out of hand. "You're a princess."

She blinked at him. "Princesses can't be secretaries?"

"No." As far as he was concerned he'd said the final word on the subject, and he went back to sorting through his papers.

She knew it was probably a lost cause, but she wasn't ready to abandon it just because he hated the idea. There were lots of things about it that appealed to her pretty strongly. And, anyway, anything was better than marrying Alphie.

"Wouldn't it be fun, though?" she said, walking toward the window. "I mean, I'd be there all the time, and you could keep track of me and be sure I wasn't getting into mischief. When you went to meetings I would be there with my laptop, typing away. Then we could go to lunch, maybe at a five star restaurant, and…"

"No." He was watching her. How could he help it? And it was hard to keep the affectionate amusement he felt toward her transparent act from showing in his face.

She frowned at him, tapping her foot in frustration. "I think I'd make a much better secretary than I do a princess," she pointed out. "You should want to encourage me to follow where my talents lie."

"Your secretarial talents seem to tend toward early lunch in nice restaurants," he noted wryly.

"I mentioned typing, didn't I?"

"You mentioned it. But I've never seen any evidence of skill in that direction."

"Maybe you should have read some of my letters," she pointed out triumphantly.

He had to laugh. She had him there. But he sobered quickly, looking at her and shaking his head. "You don't even know what is involved in being a princess," he said. "You don't have a clue. I'm just beginning to realize that no one has ever shown you what being royal is all about."

She looked at him archly. "Wasn't that *your* job?"

He sat back and stared at her, realizing the truth of her accusation. "Maybe. Yes, maybe so."

She resumed walking about the room, though she was aware of his gaze following her everywhere she went.

"So far I haven't seen a lot of advantage to being a princess," she said over her shoulder. "There are a lot of rules to follow. Everyone seems to have an opinion on how you should behave at any given moment, and I never seem to be doing it right."

"So what's the plan, Julienne?" he asked her. "If you do manage to escape my evil clutches and get across the border, where will you go? What will you do?"

She turned to look at him. "I'm hoping it won't come to that," she said earnestly. "It would be so much better if you would just understand and take my side and…and maybe we could fix things so I wouldn't have to run."

She stared into his eyes and he stared back.

"It won't work," he said at last. "Everything we've fought for these last ten years would be destroyed. It just won't work."

She stood before him with her hands out, palms up, as though offering him something from her soul but not sure how to give it to him. She didn't speak, but her eyes were pleading with him to find a way. Some way out.

CHAPTER FOUR

PRINCE ANDRE heard something at his door. He'd only been asleep for ten minutes or so and he was wide awake again in an instant. He went up on one elbow.

"Andre?"

It was Julienne, who should be asleep in the next room and not here, waking him. His first impulse was to tell her to go back to bed. Midnight meetings were way too dangerous to play around with. But maybe something was wrong. He had to find out.

"What is it?" he asked.

"Can I come in?"

He sighed. He should turn her down. He should tell her they would talk about whatever was going on with her in the morning. But he knew he wasn't going to do that. He couldn't.

"Yes, come on in. It's not locked."

The door opened and there she stood, her lovely form silhouetted by the living room light that made her night-gown disappear and left only a perfect view of her soft curves. His mouth went dry. Closing his eyes, he muttered an oath, and when that didn't help he added a small, intense prayer.

But she came in anyway.

"Andre, I can't sleep. This may be the last time we're together like this. And I have to know something."

"Okay," he said, his voice strained and grainy. "Shoot."

He was sitting up in the bed, his bare torso gleaming in the moonlight. She slid down to sit on the edge of the bed—so close—too close. He bit his lower lip, hard. Maybe pure pain would save him.

"We used to be friends," she was saying softly. "I used to count on you for…a lot of things. Including emotional support."

"I…yes," he said lamely.

"You were so important to me. After my parents died it seemed like you were all I had in the world."

He could hear the emotion in her voice and knew he had to do something to comfort her. He took her hand in his and held it tightly. "I know," he said softly. "Julienne, I know."

She drew in a shaky breath. "So why did you desert me?" she asked, her voice breaking. "Why didn't you come to visit me these last two years and more?"

He brought her hand to his lips and kissed it, closing his eyes and wishing he could take her in his arms. She was so lovely and so close and he could feel her unhappiness. "I…I couldn't come," he told her lamely. "I had to stay away."

She frowned, uncomprehending. "But why?"

He cupped her cheek with his free hand. Her hair was silver in the moonlight. "Do I really have to explain it to you?" he said, his voice rough as sandpaper.

"Yes." She came closer. "I'm just not sure…"

He took her shoulders in his hands and faced her. "I wanted to come. Julienne, you know I wanted to."

"Then why?" She searched the darkness of his eyes. "Did I do something to make you angry?"

"Angry?" He groaned. "Never."

"Then why? Do you know how heartbroken I was when you stopped coming to see me?"

"Julienne…"

"Why?"

He drew air deep into his lungs and tried to explain. "Don't you see? I had to stay away…because…because of this." He took her chin in his hand and pulled her close, touching his lips to hers. Her lips parted right away and his tongue didn't hesitate. He'd only meant to kiss her softly, but the invitation she presented was asking for more, and his body was so ready to bring it. She pressed herself to him and he pulled her even closer, so that he could feel her full breasts against his chest. The nipples were so high and hard he felt them through the light cloth of her nightgown, making him gasp. Every part of him ached for her, and it took every bit of his will and strength to pull away.

For a moment, struggling for breath, he couldn't speak. He had to get her out of here.

"Now, get back to bed before we both do something we'll regret," he told her roughly, hoping she didn't hear the thinly veiled panic in his voice.

"I wouldn't regret anything I ever did with you," she said with a sigh of yearning. Reaching out in the gloom, she flattened her hand against his naked chest.

"Julienne…" Her name sounded as though it had been ripped from his throat. He took her hand and pulled it away. "Go back where you belong."

"Okay," she said, rising reluctantly. She started away, then looked back. "That was lovely," she said breathlessly. "Alphonso kisses like a baby seal."

She left, closing the door, and Andre put his pillow over his head and tried to muffle the groan.

* * *

"Julienne." He shook her shoulder gently, then, when she didn't respond, a bit more firmly. "Wake up."

She stretched and smiled at him sleepily, only half awake.

"Andre?" she whispered, and then she reached for him.

Looking down at her beautiful sleepy face, he suddenly felt as though he'd just leapt off a tall cliff and was plunging through space. Everything in him wanted to reach for her and hold her close, wrapping himself in her body. Turning away abruptly, he fought it and won—one more time.

"Wake up," he said again, roughly this time. "We've got to get out of here."

Her eyes opened widely and she sat up, holding her covers to her chest. "What's happened?" she asked, fully awake now and thinking clearly.

"I just had a call from Security. Someone has either realized who you are or made a lucky guess. Rumors are flying. It's known that you've left the convent. That makes people wonder what is going on, as your wedding is only days away. Some of the young hot-heads from the Rubiat family are said to be coming this way to find out. Meanwhile the paparazzi are gathering like the vultures they are."

"Uh-oh." She knew exactly what that meant. This was the very unruly bunch that all the plans and schemes revolved around. If you couldn't keep the Rubiats happy, bad things happened.

"Exactly. We need to slip away before they get here." He looked at her candidly. "Are you game for making a run for it with me?"

"Am I?" Her eyes gleamed. Didn't he understand anything about her at all? "Of course. It's what I've been living for."

He wasn't sure he got that, but there wasn't time to quibble. "We've got a couple of hours before sunrise. Let's make the most of them."

He gave her a simple canvas bag to use for packing some of her new clothes and warned her to limit herself to three items.

"We won't have room for much," he said. "We'll be traveling on a big old Harley Davidson."

"A motorcycle?" she said in surprise.

He nodded. "They won't be expecting that. We'll be able to sail right past them." He looked her over quickly. "Tie your hair back with something that covers the color," he advised. "And wear jeans."

She did as he had suggested, feeling oddly excited. He went into his room to change, and when he came back she gasped. She hardly recognized this tough-looking man with a swagger and a leather jacket. He had on a pair of large aviator sunglasses and had slicked his hair back.

"Wow," she said, feeling a bit shy and tongue-tied.

"That's your favorite word, isn't it?" he mentioned, teasing her. He found a smaller, more stylish leather jacket among the clothes on her rack and handed it to her. "Here. You'll need it. We're going up into the mountains."

"Into the mountains?" On the back of a motorcycle, holding on to Prince Andre for dear life. This went beyond anything she'd ever dreamed of.

They were ready in moments, and in the elevator, heading down. But before they reached ground level Prince Andre pushed a button, and suddenly they were emerging into a stairway down to a tunnel that seemed to wind its way through the inner workings of the building. After walking for what seemed like miles, they reached a parking garage Julienne knew must be far from their starting point. He led her through a series of small rooms, and finally there was the Harley.

All black paint and chrome, it gleamed like something alive and aware, and she shivered a little, looking at it. But before long she was riding that same scary machine, and just as she'd supposed she had her arms wrapped around Andre. It was purely heaven.

Andre was feeling the spirit as well. It was amazing how free one could feel, flying across the pavement on a huge motorcycle. And with Julienne hanging on, her hands making themselves noticed around his torso—what could be better?

By now the driver at the convent would have told them she was missing. Mother Superior was probably terrified of telling him. He ought to put her out of her misery. But he would let Rolfo deal with all of that.

Dawn was just breaking as they left the city, climbing higher and higher into the surrounding mountains. They found a small roadside store and stopped to ask if there was a place to get breakfast. The storekeeper had a small kitchen in the back, and he whipped them up eggs and country sausage served in a flatbread wrap.

"Delicious," Julienne declared, and then she pestered the storekeeper until he finally divulged the secret seasonings he had used.

She made Andre laugh. A princess who cared about cooking. Unique. Watching her, he thought of what had happened the night before, how her tremulous visit had turned into a kiss that had shown his hand like nothing else could. Did she remember? Did she think of it? Or was it just another passing experience in her young life, something of a stepping stone to her full adulthood? He wasn't sure. If only things were different he would take her right now and hold her in his arms and never let her go. But things were what they were, and that was more than impossible. It would be treason.

"Where is it that we're going?" she asked him as they prepared to take off again.

"Ultimately the lake house," he said, glancing around the parking area to make sure no one could overhear him. "But first we're going to visit my cousin Giselle. You may not remember her."

She shook her head, trying to think but not coming up with anyone. "The name sounds a bit familiar, but…"

"She's Alphonso's half-sister."

"What? I didn't know Alphie had a sister."

"Different mothers," he said shortly. "Twelve years ago she was the most famous princess in the Western world. The papers were full of stories about her. She had suitors from all over—royalty, movie stars, rich industrialists. She was so beautiful, so accomplished." He smiled, remembering how stunning she'd been. Those had been happy days. But happy days never lasted long in Gemania.

"And," he added, "she was one of my best friends."

That got her attention. "What happened to her?"

He held her gaze steadily with his own. "She threw it all away. Just the way you want to. She married a starving artist, a nobody, a man who never did become successful." He shrugged. "Her father disowned her. She gave up being a princess. And now she knows what it is like to be a commoner, with no money, no connections. No help from the people who loved her."

Julienne felt the tragedy of poor Giselle's situation deeply. She could identify with it in every way.

"But she has love," she said hopefully.

"You can't eat love," he told her cynically. "It won't pay the rent." He shrugged again. "The last time I saw her the man she'd married was gone. He left her with three little children to take care of on her own." He let that sink in, watching as her eyes clouded, and then he added, "She's had it pretty rough."

Julienne thought about that for a long moment and frowned at him. "Haven't you tried to help her? You said she was your friend."

"Of course I've tried to help her. She's too proud to accept anything from me. She knows she turned her back on all of us when she made her choice, and she's living with the consequences." He watched her steadily. He was piling it on a bit thick, but it had to be done. If Giselle's story could help turn Julienne around, it would all be for a good cause.

Yeah, what a cause. He was heartsick when he thought of it. He had to make her marry another man in order to save his beloved country from war. Great. And what did that leave him? Not a hell of a lot.

But it had to be done. The country had to be his highest priority.

Thinking about Giselle, Julienne was developing a lump in her throat. "I would help her anyway!" she insisted. "In fact, I'm an adult now. It's time for me to have a living of my own. *I'll* help her. I will!"

"Really?" He felt almost cruel doing this, but it had to be done. "How can you help her if you aren't a princess anymore?"

She drew her breath in, knowing he thought he'd trapped her. Well, let him think so. She would find a way.

"I haven't been to see her for a few years, but Rolfo got word to her that we were coming. She'll be expecting us."

"And why, exactly, are you taking me to see her?"

He turned to look at her, hoping she understood his basic motive was to make things easier for her, every time. "I think you've figured that out for yourself. I want you to see her and the conditions she's living under since she gave up being a princess."

"A cautionary tale, is it?"

"Pretty much."

She was quiet as they rode through the villages, going higher and higher into the mountains. Of course she knew what he was doing. He planned to show her that choosing poverty over royal life was fraught with peril and ugliness and heartbreak. And he was probably right. But what choice did she have? Life with Alphonso promised to be much the same.

They pulled off the main road about an hour later, so that Andre could show her a meadow back in the interior— a place where he'd camped as a boy. Red and yellow wildflowers littered the valley floor, leading up to a waterfall with a huge drop, making for a magical view. They stood beside the parked bike and took it all in.

"Gorgeous," Julienne said. "I've never seen anything more special."

He smiled and looked at her, thinking she was pretty special herself. It was amazing how happy it made him just to have her appreciate something that he loved. But then, it was amazing how happy it made him just to be with her.

But any chance of that would soon be over. In just a few days she would be married to Alphonso—come hell or high water. It had to be.

The meadow was so beautiful they found they didn't want to leave it, and they walked down the path until they found a small stream. Sitting beside it, each on their own flat rock, they talked and teased each other, and just generally made the day last a little longer than they had planned.

And finally Andre got down to business.

"All right, Julienne, since you have all this worked out,

tell me what you think you're going to do with your life. If you get your wish and don't have to marry Alphonso, what will your life be like?"

Suddenly she was nervous. She hadn't told him her plans and she knew he wouldn't approve. "Well, I'd rather not go back to the convent," she said, stalling for time. "I think I'm ready to move beyond that."

"Agreed." He looked at her levelly. "But you are rejecting life as a princess, rejecting poor old Alphonso, and I want to know what you see for yourself instead. What is it that you have your heart set on? What is it that you would most like to do?"

Could she tell him? She glanced his way and decided against it. He would never understand.

"For a start, I want to learn how to drive," she said, avoiding the issue altogether.

"Didn't anyone teach you that?" No mobile phone, no driver's license—what sort of modern woman was this?

"No. You know very well there are no cars at the convent. Except Popov's, of course. And even if there were, they wouldn't teach me. They were too afraid I'd run off as soon as I had a way to do it."

He waved that away. He really didn't want to delve into it. "Okay, you want to learn to drive. That's easy enough. I could teach you in an afternoon." His look was penetrating. "Then what?"

She avoided his gaze. "What do you mean?" she said evasively.

"I mean, what is it that you want to do, Julienne? What passion calls to you?"

Should she tell him? She looked at him sideways and scrunched up her face, ready to do the dirty deed. She knew he would never look at her the same way again once she'd admitted her passion to him.

"Okay. Here it is." She took a deep breath. "I…I want to go to pastry school."

He blinked, not sure he'd heard her correctly. He leaned closer. "What kind of school?"

She looked up at him, baleful. "Pastry."

He shook his head, still at sea. "I don't understand."

Now he was starting to annoy her. Didn't understand! *Hah!*

"Peach tarts. Napoleons. Eclairs." She was facing him now, her passion expressed clearly in her face. "I want to learn to make them. I want to create new forms. I want to—"

"Enough," he said shortly, holding up his hand. He was finally getting the picture, and the picture filled him with horror. "You're trying to tell me you would rather slave away in a hot kitchen all day than be a princess? You actually expect me to believe that?"

Her shoulders sagged. "Believe what you want," she said sadly. "You asked me to tell you my passion, and I told you." She turned away. "Let's change the subject."

He knew he'd hurt her feelings, but he still couldn't believe it. They sat in silence for a few minutes, then he tried again. This time he told himself he would remain calm.

"Tell me how all this came about. What made you fall in love with the idea of being a pastry chef?"

"I love good pastry. Who doesn't?"

"Yes. Well, I love a good steak, too, but I don't plan to be a cowboy."

She rose and turned away. "Let's just go."

"No." He rose as well, taking her by the shoulders, stopping her and gazing down into her pretty face. "I want to know how it all began. Please tell me."

She searched his eyes. Could she trust him? But how could she not?

"Okay," she said slowly. They began to walk along the stream, back toward where the motorcycle was parked. "I guess it all began when Nooma, the cook at the castle, began to let me help her in the kitchen."

He frowned, wondering if the woman should be fired. "Did she do this often?" he asked.

"Often? Yes, it was often. But it was my doing, not hers." Her quick humor was back and she laughed at him. "What do you think I was doing all those long winter days, waiting for you to show up?"

He didn't laugh back. "I expected you to be improving your mind with worthy reading, learning to play the piano, practicing your French…."

"Well, I wasn't doing much of that. I was in the kitchen, baking pies."

He frowned. "Where was my aunt, the Duchess, during all this? I thought she was keeping a firm hand in your development."

She shook her head. She was going to have to rat on the lady, but she guessed it didn't matter. She'd long ago moved to the coast of France. "Your aunt, the Duchess, was usually confined to her room with a headache and a bottle of vermouth most days until teatime."

He stared at her, aghast. "Are you serious? Why didn't you tell me about that?"

"Because I wanted to be in the kitchen, not reciting lessons to the Duchess. It worked out better for both of us. She had her thing. I had mine."

He groaned. Guilt was piling up all around him. If he'd thought about it he would have realized the Duchess wasn't living up to her agreements. But he was as bad as Julienne. When he came to the castle, he'd wanted to be with her, not quizzing the Duchess to see if she had been a hard enough taskmaster.

"Oh, don't worry. I had my lessons with the governess in the morning. I got plenty done."

"Well, I guess that's a relief."

"And then I went to the convent. At first they wouldn't let me into the kitchen at all. But about six months into my stay the convent cook came down with hives and someone had to take over the cooking. The next thing you know I was in there, baking away." She smiled, remembering. Happy memories. "When I volunteered they were all relieved, and even after she got over the hives and came back she was glad to have my help in the kitchen. She taught me a lot."

He was shaking his head. "No one ever told me."

"No? Why should they?" She threw him a scathing look. "By that time you'd decided to wash your hands of me."

"Don't be ridiculous."

"I'm only taking off the rose-colored glasses and facing reality. You stayed away. You left me to my own devices. What did you expect? You're just lucky I didn't decide to become a bomb-throwing Marxist. Plenty of royals are into that these days."

That made him smile, and that was a relief. Life was better when the Prince was smiling.

She remembered how it had been when she'd first come to the Diamante castle to live after her parents had died. At first she'd been afraid of him. He'd seemed so tall, so strong—so unsmiling. But then she'd become more comfortable around him and their relationship had blossomed into something close to friendship.

He'd made it a point to eat at least one meal with her a day when he was at home in the castle—just the two of them. Those were the times she really treasured. She'd had to sit through a hundred stern lectures about how she should behave, but it was worth it. When the lecture was over, his hard, handsome face would soften with affection and he would ask her how her day had gone, or what she'd learned from her governess, or they would take the horses out and ride over the hills. He was wonderful. He was her life.

That all changed when she turned eighteen. He authorized a big party for her birthday. Her aunt invited a hundred young people from royal and noble families. There were afternoon games and then a sumptuous feast in the great hall, and finally a ball that lived up to all her fantasies. Even now, when she closed her eyes, it all came back to her—the swirling lights, the throbbing music, the excitement, the colors. The young men had all wanted to dance with her and the young women wanted to be her friend. For the first time in her life she was the center of it all. It was intoxicating—a magical night.

But best of all was the last dance at midnight. And that dance, of course, was with the Prince.

She still remembered the song that had been playing— "The Look of Love". They had swayed together without either of them saying a word, and she'd felt as though she'd entered a dream. They were out on the terrace, away from all the others. There was moonlight, shadows and music— and a gorgeous man in her arms. The song began to fade away and she looked up, yearning toward him. His mouth was there, and then the kiss. Slow and deep and delicious, it awakened senses in her body she hadn't known she had. And then he pulled away, and others surged out onto the terrace, and it was over.

But everything changed after that.

She had to admit she'd had her daydreams, even though she knew there was no reason for it. Thinking of that now, she sighed and sank against the back of his leather jacket, holding on to him as though she could hold on to the dream as well.

They entered the peaceful valley that led to Giselle's home about an hour later. Andre was looking forward to seeing her. She'd always been his favorite cousin.

He remembered when she'd come to him for advice. What had he told her? He tried to think of his words at the time. Something about not being foolish, not to count on anyone else in this world. Love didn't last. She was going to throw away everything for the chance to reach for something that would melt away like a snowflake once she'd grasped it.

She'd laughed at him, called him cynical. Was she laughing now? They would see the answer to that one soon enough. He only hoped Giselle would be ready to tell the truth to them both.

Julienne could sense his moodiness. Was she really as attuned to his emotions as it felt like she was—or was she fooling herself? She thought of all those long, lonely nights when she'd stared at the ceiling of her small cell in the convent and thought about the Prince. And all the waiting she'd done. That really was the hardest part, as hope slowly faded.

And now here she was, holding on to him with both hands. It was glorious, and she meant to savor every second of it.

CHAPTER FIVE

THE big Harley made a lot of noise driving into the valley—an excessive amount of noise for people trying to hide from too much attention, in Julienne's mind. She had a feeling Andre had been looking for an excuse to ride it out into the countryside. But she had to admit she was enjoying the trip as well.

As they neared the cottage where Giselle lived they stopped at a corner, and a young girl suddenly swung down, hanging off a branch on a tree before them.

About nine years old, she was wearing ragged jeans and a yellow pullover with a faded picture of a monkey on the chest. She stared at them from under a curly mop of light brown hair and they stared back. Andre cut the engine and swung off the bike, ready to catch her in case she should fall, but not wanting to be too obvious about it.

She let go just before he got into place, and landed on her bare feet all on her own. He grinned at her.

"Are you one of Giselle's girls?" he asked at last.

The child nodded solemnly.

He grinned at her again. "What do you know? For a moment there I thought you might be Tom Sawyer."

"Andre!" Julienne remonstrated.

"I'm Lily," she said. "Are you the Prince?"

"Yes, I am." He bowed low to her. "At your service."

Her dark eyes took him in and seemed to approve. "Mother says I can be a princess if I want to be."

"Do you want to?"

She made a face. "Heck, no. They have to sit on silk pillows and eat yucky food and wear frilly pink dresses that stick out."

He exchanged a quick look with Julienne and both of them tried not to laugh.

"Is that what your mother told you?" he asked her.

"Uh-uh." She shook her head. "I read it in a book."

"Well, I'm here to tell you right now your mother didn't spend a lot of time sitting around on silk pillows when she was your age. And, while it lasted, your mother made a wonderful princess."

Lily seemed pleased with that. "But she didn't like it. She told me she didn't ever want to be one. And I don't either."

"No frilly dresses for you, huh?"

She shook her head emphatically. "I like my clothes just fine," she said, kicking the dirt with her bare foot.

Andre gave Julienne a significant look that she knew was meant to convey how sad this was for Giselle, who must be regretting what she'd given up every day. And he might be right. But that didn't mean Julienne would regret giving up the royalty business. She wasn't Giselle.

"Hey, Your Highness," Lily was saying, looking over the chrome and black beast before her. "I sure would like a ride on that motorcycle."

"Uh…" Andre looked at Julienne and she waved her permission, jumping down herself.

"Go ahead. Give her a ride. Take her on in. I can walk. In fact, I'd like to. It's so pretty in this valley. Let me take some time to enjoy it." She handed over her helmet to the little girl and started off.

The snow pack had been a good one this year, and the

wild flowers were taking advantage of all the extra runoff water. The entire valley was a riot of color.

She laughed as she watched Andre take Lily for a tour through the village, giving her a thrill with a couple of little wheelies while he was at it. Those elicited shrieks of happy excitement from Lily.

Before she arrived at the cottage at the bottom of the hill a woman emerged from inside and waved at her. Probably in her mid-thirties, she had a full, sensual beauty that looked a bit careworn but must have been something spectacular when she was younger.

"Hello," she called out. "You must be Princess Julienne. Welcome! We're so glad to see you."

Andre arrived with Lily in tow, and two other little girls gathered around, begging for a ride as well.

"After lunch," Giselle told them. "We've got salad and finger sandwiches. The girls made the sandwiches themselves."

Going into the cottage, they all sat down around a large table. The sandwiches were free-form, as you would expect when such young ones did the cutting. But everything was great—in a homespun way.

But as Julienne began to look around the room she began to notice something. Everything was very simple, but there was a spare elegance to it that bespoke something other than poverty. As she studied her surroundings she noted more and more items that were first-quality and looked very expensive. One way or another, this family was doing quite well for itself.

But Andre didn't seem to have noticed.

"Whatever happened to…what was his name? Tavist?" he asked his cousin.

"Tavert?" Giselle looked at him, bemused. "You mean my husband?"

Andre looked surprised. "Was that his name?"

"It was, and it still is." Giselle grinned at him.

"Oh. I thought he was gone?"

"He is gone, but he'll be back. He's in Paris right now, negotiating with a major distributor."

Andre was looking more and more confused. "A major distributor? Of what?"

"Garden decor. Mainly statuary. You didn't notice on your way in?"

She led them to the window and pointed out the many fantasy creatures inhabiting the yard, from unicorns to geese to garden gnomes.

"We started experimenting with cement forms and casting from our own designs. We sold a few in our little shop, but things didn't really take off until we started selling on the internet. Now we have customers from all over the world."

They chatted a while longer, and Julienne hoped that Andre was coming to terms with the fact that his cousin's life hadn't been completely ruined after all.

"So you're still happy with the choice you made?" Julienne asked Giselle when she got a chance to talk to her privately. Andre was giving the girls turns at riding around the block on the motorcycle.

"Absolutely. The best thing I ever did."

"You ought to let Andre know. He thinks you made a big mistake."

Very quickly she explained about Alphonso, and how Andre was trying to convince her to marry him willingly. Giselle listened to the whole story, asked a few questions about the background and the treaty, then shook her head.

"Julienne, you do understand that the only reason you were paired with Alphonso was that Andre was already betrothed to that Italian princess?" she said, bringing up something Julienne had never heard a hint of before. She wondered if she'd heard what she thought she had.

"Wh…what?"

"You didn't know that?"

"Italian princess?"

"Yes. And, believe me, he wasn't ready to get married at the time. This was almost eight years ago. He fought it hard, but his father, King Harold, insisted he had to do it for the good of the country. And I have to admit Andre is all about duty and the country. He's the essence of the patriot. He finally agreed to do it."

"No! No one ever told me." Julienne shook her head, stunned. "But he never did get married, did he? What happened to her?"

"She died. It was very sad."

And Andre was back, so their conversation ended. But the revelation was shocking to Julienne and she couldn't stop thinking about it. Was it true? Giselle had intimated that she might have been paired with Andre instead of Alphonso if the timing had been right. The very concept took her breath away.

"We'd better get going," Andre was saying. "We want to make it to the lake house before dark."

"Ah, you're going to the lake house?" Giselle shook her head with a bemused smile. "So many happy summer memories, so many years ago."

Looking at her, he realized the current practices his family engaged in needed updating. Why not invite Giselle and her girls to the lake house? Why not let a new generation start building those happy memories for themselves? It wasn't as though she was the enemy, just because she'd reached for something else out of life.

But he couldn't make policy on his own. He would need the King's approval. That was something he was going to have to look into once this wedding situation had settled down. Still, he couldn't help mentioning it and suggesting he was going to talk to his father. Seeing his cousin with her girls, he knew they were exactly what the lake house was meant to host.

"We do need a vacation," Giselle admitted. "We are working much too hard. We're going to have to figure out some way to take some time off. But at least we're here and we're together and we have our girls with us all the time. I couldn't ask for a better life."

Andre looked skeptical, but he didn't challenge her on it.

As they were preparing to leave, Giselle came up to give Julienne a personal farewell.

"Julienne, you're so beautiful. Your decision must involve both your heart and your head. The heart shows us the path to joy; the head shows us the way to wisdom. You need both to find happiness."

"Thank you so much." The two women shared a warm hug. "And I hope to see you and your family again soon."

A moment later they were back roaring across the countryside, but they hadn't gone far before Andre called back a message.

"We're going to take a short detour," he told her, pulling to a stop at a crossroad intersection.

"What kind of detour?"

"I want you to see the mining district. The fountain of our country's wealth."

"Oh."

They rode over dirt and rutted roads, breathing dust and bouncing painfully. And finally they reached a lookout point where they could gaze down at the mining activity below. Huge gashes in the earth made way for big trucks and men with handcarts. It was a beehive of activity.

"There you see it," Andre told her. "The backbone of our economy, the foundation of our royal houses, the reason we've gone to war with each other through the centuries. It all comes down to wealth and power, as always."

"But there is peace right now," she said.

"And that peace is based on a balance of power between the Royal Houses that depends on you marrying Alphonso. If the Rubiats sense a weakness in our commitment to getting that done, they'll attack again. It's just what they do."

She sighed. It always came back to that. "Why don't I have to marry someone in the Rubiat family?" she asked out of curiosity.

"They don't have anyone who is right for you to marry. They haven't been able to produce a successful new generation in a long time. That's why they have to pick fights to get their way."

She looked down at all the miners, working so busily. "Is it all gemstones?" she asked him.

"Not at all. Much of the mineral material is actually used in technological and industrial ways. The gems are only the flashy, public relations side of the industry."

"The fun stuff?"

"Exactly." He turned to look at where she sat behind him on the bike. "And this is a big part of your legacy."

Her legacy. What a tiresome phrase that was getting to be. Right along with "her destiny." But she didn't talk back, and soon they were on their way again. She was growing more and more excited. She'd always loved the lake house, but for the last few years it had been so disappointing to go during the summer, be told Andre would surely come this time, and wait and wait, only to be forgotten again.

And then, finally, it was just ahead, a huge old brooding house, filled with comfortable rooms and memories, the place where everyone came eventually, every summer. It was late. The light was fading. She hugged Andre tightly as they rode up to the door. At last they were home.

CHAPTER SIX

THE morning dawned like Christmas, with a gift in every scene. There was the sunlight on the lake, the sound of birds flying by, the scent of spring flowers in the air, the prospect of a ride out on the water in a rowboat, just the two of them.

It was early in the season and there were no servants yet, no other inhabitants to spoil the fun. In just a week or two the place would be crawling with royals and their staffs. But for now they had the place to themselves.

Julienne cooked a nice breakfast of Belgian waffles and cinnamon syrup—totally delicious, if she did say herself, but Andre didn't comment. That either meant he hadn't noticed, or that he didn't want to encourage her interest by letting her know how good she was. She couldn't quite decide which it might be.

They took a walk through the orchard, with its peach trees just setting fruit, then down along the water, skipping stones and laughing at each other. Andre went out to survey some broken fenceposts he'd noticed as they rode in, and Julienne went exploring in the house.

Every room seemed to have a treasure trove of mementoes from past summers. She found amazing things everywhere, and then she pulled a beautifully bound copy of *The Highwayman* from the shelf. The Alfred Noyes

poem about the tragic love between a robber and a land-
lord's black-eyed daughter had always been a favorite of
hers, and she opened the book, prepared for a treat. But
the first thing she saw was that the flyleaf had been torn
out, as though someone wanted to either preserve or destroy whatever was written there. She frowned, then noticed there were indentations on the next page. A note had
been written, and with enough pressure to leave a pretty
good impression. Searching a nearby desk, she found a
pencil and proceeded to shade it lightly across the perti-
nent area. The missing note sprang into view.

"Hah!" She couldn't help but give a little crow of vic-
tory. Then she put down her pencil and attempted to read
the note.

"My darling A," it began.

She bit her lip, wondering if it had been written to
Andre.

You are my Highwayman, and, like Bess, I'll be
waiting by moonlight. Your first love, your true
love, Denise.

She stared at the note. Now she was certain it was meant
for Andre. Her teeth began to chatter, and it was a moment
before she realized she was trembling. She shook her head,
trying to shake it off. How silly of her. Of course he'd had
women who'd adored him. Who knew how old this was?
What did she expect?

And yet somehow it just got into her heart and twisted
it. Pure pain. Jealousy? Maybe. Why not? Of course it hurt
to think of him with another woman, no matter how silly
that was.

Clasping the book to her chest, she went in search of

him and found him, just back from his trip around the estate.

"Who's Denise?" she asked bluntly, not waiting on niceties.

"Denise?" He frowned, then his brow cleared. "Oh, Denise." He glanced at her quickly, his eyes sharpening. "What do you know about Denise?"

"I found this book." She held it out to him. "It looks like she dedicated it to you."

"Ah." He smiled, then quickly erased it.

"Did you love her?"

He rose slowly, turning away and looking out into the sky. "I thought I loved her. She was very beautiful. I was very young." Turning back, he met her gaze candidly. "We were both young, and we were thrown together, and we did what young people do." He hesitated, then shook his head ruefully. "Okay, here's what happened. Her father was the lake house butler. A summer romance. It was over by the time the leaves turned."

She stared at him, but what she saw was the entire story playing out in her head.

Summer magic.

"Did you want to marry her?"

"Marry her? Why would I want to marry her?"

"Ah, yes. She was the butler's daughter." Julienne made a significant face.

But he laughed at her. "Julienne, you're too old to live in a dream world. Face facts. We didn't make the world the way it is and we can't do much to change it. We are royal. We have to follow a certain path in life. Live with it."

She felt her lower lip coming out in rebellion. "No."

He shook his head, not sure what she meant. "What do you mean, no?"

She flashed him a look. "I think you know what I mean. I won't do it."

So she was talking about the Alphonso thing again. He gritted his teeth in annoyance. "The hell you won't."

She glared at him, then flounced off to sulk in the kitchen. And while she was there she whipped up a pan of delectable pastries such as he had never had before. He ate a few, then ate a few more, and had to admit she had the knack. But he still wouldn't give her the satisfaction of hearing it aloud.

"Tell me what happened with the butler's daughter," she coaxed, once he was full of pastry and groaning with pleasure.

He looked at her and shook his head. "Okay, Julienne. Here goes. I was crazy about her that summer. She was gorgeous, with thick red hair and a wide red mouth that just begged to be kissed."

Julienne turned away, biting her lip and hating this. Too much information. But she had to know.

"We pledged to meet in the fall in Cairns," he said. "I was going to university there. She was going to dental assistant school. I got to town early and raced over to find her apartment, hoping to surprise her. And there she was, in bed with some skinny grad student." He shrugged. "The end. She betrayed me and I never saw her again."

"She betrayed you?" She had a flash of intuition. Was this one of the seeds of his cynicism about love, about marriage? Could be.

He grimaced. "Well, it was hardly fair to even call it that. Looking back, I saw that she realized sooner than I did that it was never going to work. Only pain and unhappiness could result. It was time to move on, and she did just that."

Suddenly he realized that she'd come up next to him and was lacing her fingers with his.

"I'm sorry," she said, her eyes huge and dark with sadness. "I'm so sorry your heart was broken."

He meant to laugh at her, to tell her how naive she was being, but something in those big brown eyes wouldn't let him. Instead, he just smiled and let her comfort him.

Looking at her, he was reminded of the feeling he sometimes had as his work-weary gaze settled on a rolling green lawn. A calm serenity seemed to gather around her like a haze, and then her face would turn his way, her eyes sparkling with mischief, and he would think of her as a spray of colorful wild flowers dancing in a spring breeze instead. It just made him happy to look at her.

What a contrast she was to the life he'd been living, with all its boredom, cynicism, and backbiting treachery—the sort of thing he had to deal with every day. It had been exciting at first. He'd reached an important level of power early in his life and he'd used it. Now he didn't feel so powerful anymore. The excitement was gone. All that was left was the endless responsibility.

And she thought *she* was caught in a trap.

A half an hour later, they were out on the lake in the rowboat, drifting happily in the noonday sun.

"So, were you ever engaged?" she asked him out of the blue.

He thought about it for a moment.

"I guess I was. At one point, a long time ago, I was supposed to marry an Italian princess from an old royal family."

She looked at him earnestly. "But you didn't?"

"No. She died."

She nodded. "Giselle told me about it." She looked up

at him. "She also said that they would have made the betrothal between you and me instead of Alphonso if it hadn't been for your engagement to the Italian princess."

He frowned. "She shouldn't have said that. I'm not sure it's true."

She stared at him. He was so darn obstinate. "So what exactly happened to the Italian princess?"

"I only met her once, fleetingly." He frowned again, remembering things best forgotten, things he hadn't thought of for years. "She seemed very frightened," he said softly. "I always wondered…"

There was a shiver in the air between them.

"How did she die?" Julienne asked, tensing for the answer.

He looked at her, hollow-eyed. "She drowned. In the estate swimming pool. She went swimming alone late at night."

He stared into Julienne's eyes and knew they were both thinking the same thing. Did she drown on purpose? Did she love someone else? Did she hate the idea of marrying Andre so much that she would rather die than submit?

"We'll never know," he said, so softly she blinked, wondering if he'd really said it aloud or if they had both thought it. It made her catch her breath, the way they seemed to be able to invade each other's thoughts at times. Like some kind of magic. Could he really read her mind? Could he see how she really felt about him? And could he stand it?

"Will you ever marry?" she asked him.

He shook his head emphatically. "No."

His easy acceptance of that outraged her. "Why not?"

He looked at her, his eyes haunted. "The only thing that would make me marry would be if I needed to do it for the good of my country."

She winced. "Like I'm expected to do, you mean?"

"Yes. Like you."

She shook her head, laughing softly. "So you're willing to throw yourself on that grenade if it gets tossed your way? But you won't go looking for it on your own?"

He shrugged. "Something like that."

They were silent for a long moment, listening to the splash of the water lapping against the sides of the boat, and then she said, "I think you should marry. And right away, too."

He looked up at her, bemused. "Really?"

"Yes. I think you should marry for love."

He stared at her, his blue eyes hooded. "What if I don't ever love anyone?"

Did he really think she was going to buy that at this point?

"Well, that's your misfortune," she snapped. "*Try* loving someone, why don't you?"

He shook his head, half smiling at her response. "What do you know about love? You don't love anyone. Or do you?"

She threw out her hands, palms up. "Only you, my liege."

Closing his eyes, he threw back his head and sighed deeply. "I never know for sure when you're being serious," he said softly. "Tell me the truth."

"I'm being as honest as I know how," she countered quickly, wishing she dared reach for him. "Ever since my parents died you have been the one person in the world whom I adored. I clung to you, needed you…loved you."

He looked at her as though that wasn't what he'd wanted to hear. "That's a different kind of love," he said gruffly, looking away.

"Is it? I don't know. You were the center of my universe." She watched him avoid her gaze, and then went on. "And then you stopped coming to see me. You stopped answering my letters. And it was as if everything in my world died."

"Julienne!"

He stared at her, transfixed. What could he say? It was for her own good that he'd done that. He hadn't meant to hurt her. In fact he'd only meant to save her from what might happen if he saw her too much. He should have been more open about his motives. He should have explained why they were necessary. She was so young—how was she to know the dangers that could lurk in the male heart?

But he should have been more careful. He should have made sure she had someone to turn to. Looking at her now, he ached with regret.

Taking her hand in his, he looked into her eyes. "Julienne, I'm sorry," he said simply. "I didn't realize you would be so hurt by my neglect. You are so...so charming and lovely, and everyone loves you. I thought you would hardly notice if I just faded into the background and left you alone. Everyone was so enchanted by you."

She stared into his eyes, sank into their depths. "I didn't want everyone. I wanted you."

Those were the words that stuck with him as the day began to fade. She'd said it starkly. There could be no doubt as to her meaning. And yet there was nothing he could do about it. The future was set in stone.

When they were back in the house he tried to talk to her about Alphonso, about giving him a chance, about trying to like him.

"You do know he collects insects, don't you?" she told him, when she'd had about enough of his goading.

"He collects what?" He leaned closer to try to hear what she'd said.

"Insects," she said, as clearly as she could. "Those things with too many legs."

He sat back, nonplussed but interested. "Well, good. He has a scientific turn of mind."

"No." She shook her head. "It's not like that. He has them in little bottles. All over his room. With little name tags."

He shrugged. "Latin names?"

She sighed. "Andre, try to focus. There are no scientific notations on these bottles. There are names. Nicknames. Like Fred—and Cindy. Those are two beetles he introduced me to. These little bugs aren't part of an experiment. They're pets."

His face began to mirror distaste at last. "Oh, my God."

She nodded, glad he finally got it. "Well might you say so." She flipped her hair back and flashed him a look. "And you want me to marry this man."

He couldn't help it. He laughed aloud. And after a moment she laughed along with him.

"You see how impossible it is?" she challenged him.

He shook his head. "I'll talk to him," he promised. "He's young. He'll change."

"Really? Can I get that in writing?"

He didn't answer, but he didn't have to. She knew in his mind she was already as good as married to Alphie. She was going to have to begin making plans again.

She looked at him, and it was suddenly as though the sun had broken through the clouds. She understood something about him she hadn't realized before. His first allegiance was to his country. He could never be like her, ready to throw it all away and dash for the border. He loved his country, he lived for his country, and he would never do anything to harm it. To him, royalty was the life's blood of this land. Though on the surface one would think of him as a philandering playboy, the Andre inside wasn't that way at all. He was good, responsible and true—a man you could depend on. And she loved him all the more for it.

She didn't want to marry Alphonso. She hated the thought of it. But how was she going to be able to convince a man like this to let her out of her commitment? It wasn't going to happen.

The day blended seamlessly into evening. There was a cold snap in the air, and Andre built a fire in the fireplace while she prepared dinner out of canned supplies she found in the kitchen. After eating, they sat on the couch in front of the fire, each with a glass of wine, and talked softly.

"Okay, Julienne," he said grudgingly. "I have to admit it. You are a very good cook. Everything you make has some sort of special quality that raises it above normal cooking. You've got talent."

She smiled. She already knew that, but to have him notice made it so much more important.

"But as a princess of the realm," he said, "I don't know how you ever thought you could get away with going to pastry school somewhere."

She nodded. "I've thought about it long and hard," she told him. "And looked into resources. And from what I've managed to learn, I think the best thing would be to start a national culinary institute right here in Gemania." She shrugged. "If I actually had the power, I would bring the instructors to me."

He nodded. "Have you spoken to Alphonso about it?" he asked.

She stared at him, color draining from her face. Didn't he understand? Alphonso was not going to be a part of her life. It just couldn't happen. What he thought had nothing to do with her future. But there was no point in arguing about that. She didn't want to ruin their last evening together.

A bit later she watched him staring moodily into the flame and knew she was the source of his problems. She had a strong impulse to go over and take his hand, smile up at him and tell him, *It's all right. I'll do it. Anything that will make you smile again.*

But she would be lying, because it was something that she really couldn't do.

She realized now she'd had a dream in her head when she'd come looking for him. She'd thought he would look up and see her and electricity would zap between them and he would realize she really was the only one for him. She'd even gone so far as to fantasize him saying, *If I can't have you, no one can*, and then they would come together for a passionate kiss, then run off to the South Seas to live on a tropical island under assumed names. It sounded good to her. Obviously he didn't agree.

Turning toward him, she pulled her legs up under her and leaned back against the pillows.

"Do you remember when you kissed me?" she asked him.

He raised one dark eyebrow. "Do you mean last night?"

"No, not that time. At my eighteenth birthday party. The last dance."

She held her breath, watching his reaction. Did he remember? Or was it so normal for him to kiss a woman he was dancing with that the kiss she held as so special was just one of many in his mind.

He turned toward her slowly, and then he nodded, his eyes dark in the firelight. "I remember," he said softly.

She laughed with relief. "I've lived off of that kiss for three years."

Frowning, he turned away and stared into the fire.

"Well, you shouldn't have. That was the catalyst, the reason I had to stay away from you."

"Because of a kiss?"

He glanced back at her. "Because of an emotion. I knew if I was near you…." He turned away and shook his head. "Well, I think you know what would have happened."

"Do I?" she said softly. "What was it? Tell me."

He raked a hand through his thick hair, making it stand on end, and looked at her from under lowered brows.

"I don't know why you want to know all this. I don't know what it helps. But I'll be honest. I was falling in love with you. And I couldn't let that happen."

She was trembling, but not in fear. In sweet anticipation.

"Why not?"

"The treaty." He set down his wine glass and stared into her eyes. "The treaty is fundamental to peace in this country. We can't let anything ruin that."

The country. Yes, of course that was important. But for once couldn't he just look at her and let the feelings between them work? Did he always have to let the country get in the way?

"So…do you love me now?" she asked him.

He took a long time to answer. "It's not fair to ask me that."

She drew her breath in. "I take that as an affirmative."

"Take it any way you like. It doesn't change anything."

"Oh, yes it does." Reaching out, she took his hands in hers and gazed up earnestly into his eyes. "Andre, tell me true. Would you marry me if you could?"

She expected him to react badly, to pull away, to claim such a thing had never entered his mind, but to her surprise he didn't do any of those things. Instead, he looked back at her and said quietly, "I don't know. I never expect to marry anyone."

Her hands gripped his tightly. "Find a way," she begged him. "Oh, please, Andre. Find a way."

He didn't promise to do that, but he did lean toward her. This time his kiss was sweet and simple. She closed her eyes and delighted in it, until he finally pulled away. And then she sighed and snuggled down into the pillows.

"I love you, Andre," she said softly, not even looking at him. "I love you with all my heart."

He didn't answer, and when she finally looked up he was gone. Tears filled her eyes, but she smiled through them. He did love her and she knew it. Now what on earth were they going to do about it?

CHAPTER SEVEN

"ANDRE, look!" Julienne cried as they turned up the long, sloping driveway to the castle. "It looks like just about everyone is here already."

The extended parking lot was filled with limousines, and servants were trundling trunks and clothing racks to and fro.

Andre pulled the Harley up to the entry colonnade. "It's not surprising," he said. "The wedding is only a few days away. And royals like to party at things like this for days at a time."

She sighed. "I was hoping we'd have some time…" Her voice trailed off and she bit her lip. Time for what? She still couldn't put it into words. "I don't know. I can't face all these people. What am I going to say to them?"

"You'll be fine, Princess," he told her, chucking her under her chin. "You'll think of something."

A sort of despair surged over her. She wasn't supposed to be here. She was supposed to be in Paris by now, checking out pastry schools.

"Andre, I only came back with you because you said…" She shook her head. Had he really said anything she could cling to? "What I mean is, I'm counting on you to come through for me this time. Don't leave me waiting at the door with no hope. Don't do that to me again."

He looked at her. A part of him was astonished. What did she expect of him? What could he do to change things? He'd never promised to release her from the treaty. He didn't have the power to do that.

And yet, looking deep into her eyes, he knew exactly what she expected. Would he be able to come through for her?

They went into the castle and the bustle was even worse inside. As they walked through the courtyard toward the dining room, where a late brunch was being served, she saw Alphonso at the other side of the fountain. She stuck her elbow in Prince Andre's ribs.

"There he is," she whispered loudly. "It's Alphie."

Andre craned his neck and shook his head. "I really don't see the resemblance myself," he told her.

She frowned. "What resemblance?"

He met her gaze sideways. "To a baby seal."

She laughed. "You haven't kissed him," she murmured as they entered the dining room.

"And I don't think I ever will."

She smiled. "Lucky you."

He smiled back and knew, suddenly, that he had to find a way to have her for his own. She seemed to be having similar thoughts.

"Andre, listen to me," she said, grabbing his arm and pulling him into a private area off the courtyard. "I'm not sure why I came back with you, because I won't marry Alphie. Don't think you'll talk me into it. I say no. I understand that you're prepared to do anything for your country. That's who you are. And I'm prepared to do a lot. But I won't do that. There has to be another way to satisfy the country—and especially the Rubiats."

She stared up at him with huge eyes.

"It's up to you to figure out what can be done," she warned him.

He covered her hand with his own. "And you're not involved?" he asked, a smile twisting his wide mouth.

"I don't have the experience and I don't know the ways of diplomacy. You've been doing it for years. Teach me, and I'll join in. I'm willing to do anything you tell me to do, short of marrying Alphie."

He stroked her lips with his forefinger and turned away. "Believe me, Julienne, I'm working on it. Just give me some time. I'll think of something."

In fact, an idea was beginning to take form in his head that might have even more advantages than appeared at first glance. He'd wanted to get out of the pretend-playboy business for quite some time. Though he'd actually left it long ago in spirit, the image remained strong. He was ready to lose that, too. Could this be a blessing in disguise?

He worked on his idea for the rest of the day. He met with Alphonso, getting to know him a bit better, and made Julienne be friendly to him. Strangely enough, the feeling he got from the younger man was out of step with what he would expect from a happy groom. He didn't seem much happier about the prospect of marrying Julienne than she did about marrying him.

"Alphonso seems out of sorts, doesn't he?" he mentioned to her that evening.

"Well, yes. Understandable, under the circumstances."

He nodded. "Perhaps he needs a little distraction. I think I'll take him down to the casino and put him up in my suite for a day or two. Would you mind?"

"Mind?" She made a face. "How about a slow boat to China? Or a trip to the moon? Or…"

He grinned at her. "I get the picture. You have no objection."

Of course she had an objection. If he took Alphonso off somewhere, that meant *he* would be gone as well. And right now she wanted to savor every moment with him she could muster. But she could see that he had a purpose in mind, and she only hoped it would develop into something that would help their situation.

So the two men left for the casino and she stayed where she was, enduring rehearsals and dress fittings and meetings with older royals who needed to be shown respect. And before she knew it the wedding day was dawning, bright and clear.

And she was in a panic. She hadn't heard from Andre. She'd expected to see him back before now. And Alphonso...where was he? What were the two of them up to? She had no way of knowing, and the hour of the ceremony was drawing closer all the time.

What was she to do? She was on a conveyor belt toward matrimony and she wasn't sure if she would be able to jump off in time to save herself. Her only hope was that Alphonso would have cold feet. If he didn't show up she would have a chance at stopping everything in its tracks and making her escape.

She went through all the preparations, feeling like a robot. Cousins and aunts and nieces all gathered round, chattering happily and helping her get ready for the biggest day of her life. She listened and answered and laughed along with them, but her mind was with Andre.

Where are you? was the refrain that kept screaming in her head. *What are you doing? What have you done with Alphonso?*

She didn't understand why no one thought it strange that the groom—and the Crown Prince—were missing.

"Oh, they'll show up," people kept telling her. "You

know Prince Andre. He always has something unusual up his sleeve."

That was all well and good, but she would feel much better about it if she had some idea of what his unusual trick was going to be this time. Here she was, watching the driveway for Andre again, just as she'd been doing for the last three years every time there was a gathering of the clan. It gave her a very sick feeling in the pit of her stomach.

"It's time, Your Highness."

It was time. She was standing in the prep room in a beautiful satin and lace gown, with flowers and seed pearls and everything else one would expect—and the groom hadn't shown up. But it was time.

A wedding march began to swell through the ancient halls. She walked out into the foyer where King Harold was waiting, stepping very carefully. The King smiled at her and said, "Quite a situation, quite a day. I'm sure you'll both be very happy." She smiled back at him, assuming he was just talking pleasantries.

Meanwhile, she was shaking like a leaf and afraid she might faint. Her only hope was that there would be no one waiting for her at the end of the aisle. Then she could turn to the crowd and shrug and say, *Oh, well! I guess we can't have a wedding today.*

But what would she do if Alphonso was waiting there? She needed an escape plan and she needed it fast.

There were too many people standing and waving and *oohing* as they passed. She couldn't see clearly toward the altar. If he was there, she would run for it. What would all these people think when they saw the bride racing for the exit? Would anyone try to stop her?

She had Popov waiting at the side entrance, just in case. He didn't know that she would be asking him to drive her all the way to the border. He no doubt thought it would be back to the convent. Would he rebel when she told him? She would have to deal with that when she came to it. Right now, her only goal was to make sure she and Alphonso never actually exchanged vows.

The crowd seemed awfully noisy. Weddings were usually quieter affairs, with the music and the minister making all the noise that needed to be made. But right now people were laughing and calling out to each other as though it were a sports event. She looked around, puzzled. What was going on?

There was someone waiting at the bottom of the long walk, waiting to marry her, but she couldn't see clearly. Was it Alphonso? Or someone who was going to call the whole thing off? Her mind was abuzz with too much sound and color. She couldn't think straight.

And then she came around the last bend and there was her groom, standing there for all the world to see. And now she saw why the room was in chaos and commotion.

She gasped, broke away from King Harold, and dashed forward, reaching out and throwing her arms around her husband to be—Prince Andre.

"What—? How—?" she babbled as she held him close, half laughing, half crying with relief.

He leaned down, smiling with all the love in the world in his eyes. The crowd was laughing and applauding, giving him cover to whisper in her ear.

"I've fixed everything," he told her. "I've announced that your engagement to Alphonso was a ruse to pave the way for your wedding to me. Alphonso is happily ensconced at the casino, taking my place there. My father and all the other princes have signed off on the changes. We're free to have a life together."

Free.

That was all she'd ever wanted.

Well, that and the most handsome prince in the land. Just those two things.

Electric with happiness, she joined him at the altar and waited for the ceremony to begin.

"I do," she said at the appropriate time, loud and clear. "Oh, yes, I do!"

* * * * *

NINA HARRINGTON
The Ordinary King

Nina Harrington grew up in rural Northumberland, England, and decided at the age of eleven that she was going to be a librarian—because then she could read *all* of the books in the public library whenever she wanted! Since then she has been a shop assistant, community pharmacist, technical writer, university lecturer, volcano walker and industrial scientist, before taking a career break to realise her dream of being a fiction writer. When she is not creating stories to make her readers smile, her hobbies are cooking, eating, enjoying good wine—and talking, for which she has had specialist training.

GET FREE BOOKS and FREE GIFTS WHEN YOU PLAY THE...

Lucky 7

Just scratch off the silver box with a coin. Then check below to see the gifts you get!

SLOT MACHINE GAME!
YES!
I have scratched off the silver box. Please send me the 2 free Harlequin® Romance books and 2 free gifts for which I qualify. I understand I am under no obligation to purchase any books, as explained on the back of this card.

❏ I prefer the regular-print edition
116/316 HDL FEFN

❏ I prefer the larger-print edition
186/386 HDL FEFN

FIRST NAME   LAST NAME

ADDRESS

APT.#   CITY

STATE/PROV.   ZIP/POSTAL CODE

7 7 7	Worth TWO FREE BOOKS plus 2 FREE Mystery Gifts!
🍒 🍒 🍒	Worth TWO FREE BOOKS!
♣ ♣ 🍒	Worth ONE FREE BOOK!
🔔 🔔 🍒	TRY AGAIN!

Visit us at: www.ReaderService.com

H-R-09/11

DETACH AND MAIL CARD TODAY!

© 2011 HARLEQUIN ENTERPRISES LIMITED
Printed in the U.S.A. ® and ™ are trademarks owned and used by the trademark owner and/or its licensee.

The Reader Service—Here's How It Works:

Accepting your 2 free books and 2 free gifts (gifts valued at approximately $10.00) places you under no obligation to buy anything. You may keep the books and gifts and return the shipping statement marked "cancel". If you do not cancel, about a month later we'll send you 6 additional books and bill you just $4.09 each for the regular-print edition or $4.59 each for the larger-print edition in the U.S. or $4.49 each for the regular-print edition or $5.24 each for the larger-print edition in Canada. That's a savings of at least 14% off the cover price. It's quite a bargain! Shipping and handling is just 50¢ per book in the U.S. and 75¢ per book in Canada.* You may cancel at any time, but if you choose to continue, every month we'll send you 6 more books, which you may either purchase at the discount price or return to us and cancel your subscription.

*Terms and prices subject to change without notice. Prices do not include applicable taxes. Sales tax applicable in N.Y. Canadian residents will be charged applicable taxes. Offer not valid in Quebec. All orders subject to credit approval. Credit or debit balances in a customer's account(s) may be offset by any other outstanding balance owed by or to the customer. Please allow 4 to 6 weeks for delivery. Offer available while quantities last.

CHAPTER ONE

'I AM so sorry, Kate, but there is still no sign of your luggage. They are chasing up the airline, but you may have to do some emergency shopping. Not, perhaps, the finest welcome to Ghana you could have had.'

Kate O'Neill smiled across at the company's PR agent for West Africa, who had already gone beyond the call of duty to try and track down her precious suitcase. 'I blame it on that five-hour delay leaving Mexico. I only just made the connecting flight out of London with minutes to spare. It was a bit optimistic to expect my bag to have done the same, but thank you for trying, Molly. I really appreciate it.'

Molly Evans sighed heavily and took a sip of her coffee. 'Fingers crossed it will turn up soon. You do know that Andy will never forgive me if I don't look after you on your first field trip to Ghana, don't you? He feels bad enough leaving you in the lurch like this at zero notice.'

'I'll be fine,' Kate answered. 'Have you heard from Andy yet? His wife was still in labour when I spoke to him yesterday from Mexico.'

Molly lowered her cup and grinned across at Kate. 'There was a text message waiting for me this morning. His twin boys are healthy, hungry and tired, just like their parents. I am so pleased for him. He has a lot of sleepless nights to look forward to, and wouldn't have it any other way. Andy has waited a long time to have the family he wanted, even if the boys did decide to make their appearance three weeks early. Good luck to him.'

Kate lifted up her coffee cup and clinked it against Molly's. 'I'll drink to that. I only hope that the delegates don't expect me to know as much about the country as Andy does. He has been here—what?—fifteen or twenty years?'

Molly nodded. 'At least. And don't worry; the organisers know that you had to step in at the very last minute.' Then Molly paused and looked at Kate over the top of her spectacles. 'Unless, of course, I can persuade you to take over from Andy on a more permanent basis?' Molly added in a casual, innocent voice, her eyebrows raised.

Kate hesitated for a moment, her mind reeling with the impact of Molly's innocent question.

Take over? Take over a job so totally engrossing and demanding that you could forget any kind of family life? Oh, no! She had seen for herself what had happened to Simon's father, and the impact his total dedication had had on his wife and son. She would not be making that same mistake.

'Ah. That would be no,' Kate replied with a warm smile. 'I am only working on the project for the next few weeks or so, while Andy is on paternity leave.'

'Your work in Mexico has been very impressive, Kate,' Molly said with a slight nod. 'We could really use someone with your experience to support the team here in Ghana, and I know that Andy has been looking for a long-term replacement for months. Why not think about it over the next few days?'

Luckily for Kate, at that moment there was a rush of chatter from the hotel reception desk as the airport shuttle bus dropped off more new delegates for the technology conference and Molly immediately started bustling together her paperwork and slurping down the last of her coffee.

'Sorry, Kate. Duty calls. Catch up with you at the welcome session. And…Kate?'

Only Kate was not listening. Her attention was totally focused on the tall, rugged-looking man in very dusty clothing who was standing in the elegant lobby, and her jaw dropped in that fraction of a second when she recognised who it was—who had just walked back into her life after three years.

A bolt of energy hit her hard in the stomach, and sucked the air from her lungs so powerfully that she had to clutch onto the edge of the table with both hands to stop herself sliding off the chair and onto the floor.

She could not believe that this was happening.

It had to be some sort of crazy nightmare, brought on by lack of sleep from two long-haul flights after a busy week and way too much caffeine to compensate.

There was nothing else that could explain this giddiness. She did not do giddy. She never did giddy.

Except that six feet two of broad-shouldered, brown-haired hunk of a man-boy from a distant country she called the past was blocking her view of the hotel entrance and the light from the halogens above his head. Even at this distance, with only a side view of his head, there was no doubt at all about who she was looking at.

It was a face she'd used to know by heart. A face she had kept in that safe locked room in her memory alongside the fading images of the people she had once loved.

But there was no mistaking him.

Simon Richard Reynolds. *Her Simon.*

The last person on the planet she had expected to see

at that moment, in this hotel, and still in Ghana after three years, took a couple of steps closer—and the sight of him sent her brain into a complete spin.

This must be what it feels like to have a heart attack.

Her hands moved instinctively to smooth down the fabric of her skirt, and she had to force herself not to check her hair and her shoes to make sure that she was clean and neat and *almost* good enough for the smartest, richest boy in her university class. It seemed that old habits were hard to break.

'Oh, there's Simon,' Molly said with a smile. 'Have you two already met?'

Met? Kate did not know whether to laugh or to cry. Her brain was racing with memories of Simon laughing, Simon racing along the beach holding her hand, Simon kissing her so hard that she thought she would die from the pleasure of it… *Her Simon.*

'Yes. We were on the same course at university back in England. But that was years ago,' she added quickly. 'I haven't seen him since. I certainly had no idea he was still in Africa.'

'He most certainly is,' Molly said with a certain lilt in her voice, 'and likely to stay in Ghana for quite some time. We're all very excited about what Simon has achieved here.'

'Really? Is he working on one of your field projects?' Kate asked as casually as she could; only it came out squeaky and a lot wobblier than she wanted.

Molly looked up at her in surprise. 'Oh, no. Simon was working with Andy. I am looking forward to his presentation this afternoon—so far it sounds like one of the company's most successful initiatives. Lucky girl—he's all yours. Now, if you will excuse me, I promise I'll catch up with you later. And welcome to Ghana, Kate. *Akwaaba.*'

Breathing was starting to become difficult.

Simon had been working with Andy? *He was all hers?*

That could not be right. She had read through the files on the three projects Andy was supervising during the long flight from Mexico, and she certainly hadn't seen Simon's name come up. Tired she might be, but she would not have missed the name which was engraved on her heart.

And then Kate sighed out loud.

Of course. *Stupid girl.*

All of the proposals for company sponsorship had to go through the most senior member of that particular small tribal kingdom in Ghana. Royal protocol demanded that only the king for the area made those sorts of decisions. Volunteers like Simon would not be listed on any of those high-level reports.

Kate's cup rattled on the saucer as the terrible reality of her situation hit home.

Suddenly it was all a bit too much. She was on a new continent, for goodness' sake, in a new country, without her luggage after a long nightmare journey from Mexico. Her body clock had no idea what time of day it was, and she was eating breakfast when she should probably be sleeping.

And now she was going to have to work with Simon Reynolds if she was going to make a go of her temporary promotion and impress her boss, just when she *needed* promotion so very badly.

Kate sucked in a lungful of air and watched Molly meet and greet the other conference delegates, dressed in bright African robes or western dress, and felt even more guilt. The company she worked for was one of the main sponsors for this conference. She should be on her feet, smiling and shaking hands like Molly and Simon were doing now. Networking. Explaining why Andy was not there to meet them as usual. Making the delegates feel welcome.

But that would mean talking to Simon. And she was not ready for that. Not yet.

How did you start a conversation when what you really wanted to say was along the lines of, *Hi, Simon—isn't the weather nice for this time of year? Oh, by the way, do you still blame me for destroying your parents' marriage and generally ruining your life? Because I would really like to know why you abandoned me just when I needed you the most and broke my heart in the process. If it is not too much trouble?*

Suddenly her confidence faltered and shuddered to a grinding halt.

Kate swallowed down the huge lump of emotion and regret in her throat that was threatening to overwhelm her. She had sworn three years ago, during that terrible summer after he left, that she would not waste one more tear or sleepless night on Simon Reynolds while her stepdad and her sister needed her to be strong for them.

She could do this. The company needed her to be a total professional and do her job. Simon was just another volunteer working on the company-sponsored rural IT project. That was all.

She was going to show him that she had changed in the past three years. Kate O'Neill was not the push-over he had known at university, who had relied on her extrovert boyfriend to make all the big decisions for them both. The tables had turned. *She* was the one making the decisions now.

Forcing her head up, she stood up from the table, smiled across to the delegates and lifted her chin, back straight.

Only at that same moment Molly said something to Simon, and they both turned their heads in her direction.

Simon's gaze met hers, locked and held.

She had always been able to read Simon from those remarkable grey eyes, but at this distance it was not possible—except for a flicker of… What? What was it she saw in that instant? Hurt? Need? Confusion? Surprise and amazement? Remorse?

Kate's stomach clenched and tied into a tight painful knot under the cold, analytical focus of his stare. Then Simon gave one hard blink and the moment was lost.

With one brief smile and half-bow to the group around him Simon turned towards her and strolled in slow, deliberate steps across the room, as though he owned the hotel, the resort and most of the world around it.

Confident. Strong. Impressive.

Simon Reynolds had been brought up to be a leader amongst men, and it showed in every step that he took—no matter where he was or what he was wearing.

In fact she might have been intimidated by him if it had not been for a few tiny aspects of his new look. The super-smart, casual but expensive preppy clothes his mother had used to buy him in London when he was a student had been replaced by a loose short-sleeved shirt made from the same type of striped fabric she had seen being worn at the airport the previous evening. The faded and darned fabric hung over the scruffiest trousers she had ever seen in her life. The knees were patched with several irregular pieces of fabric in various patterns, which seemed to have been cut out with the same nail scissors he had used to trim his hair. A brown cowhide shoulder bag was slung casually across his chest.

He was unshaven, he was trailing a line of red dust along the floor as he walked, and he looked tastier than hot bread straight from the oven.

Mouth-watering. Hot. Bread.

Perhaps he was more country Sourdough than buttery brioche, but Simon Reynolds still looked just as delicious, and her treacherous heart yearned for a taste.

Her whole body prickled to attention, aware of every move that he made.

Kate sucked in a breath, dropped her gaze, and pretended to gather together her papers on the table, trying to ignore the hot pulsing of the blood in her head as her fingers fumbled and trembled.

Then Simon took another step forward, pausing to greet a delegate on the way, and the air seemed to catch in her lungs in the form of her old nervous cough. The one she had thought she had got rid of.

She couldn't do it.

She couldn't talk to him like this in front of the other people in the room. Her emotions were too open and exposed. And her failure to control herself had hit so hard that she knew she would have to escape until she could steady herself.

A minute. That was it. She needed a minute to get her head straight before she went back to work. This time she would be the one running away from him.

Simon watched from the other side of the room as Kate quickly gathered together her paperwork and strolled out onto the hotel terrace, her back straight and her shoulders high with tension.

Kate O'Neill!

Of all the technology conferences in the entire world she had to walk into this one.

He could hardly believe it! But there could only be one tall, curvaceous, elegant blonde-haired woman called Kate O'Neill, and it had taken a single brief glance to confirm it. Katie was back in his life.

He had not even realised that she was working for the same international IT company that was sponsoring his project until an hour ago, when he had finally managed to get through to Andy and her name had echoed down the line like a bolt from above.

Andy Parsons was his contact, his friend, and his longstanding connection to the outside world from the remote rural village in the Volta area of Eastern Ghana where Simon had made his home. Andy had been a keen supporter of his work right from the first time he had met him with his dad all those years ago. Only now Andy was back in England with his new babies, and judging from the telephone conversation they'd had that morning he was so thrilled and stunned that Simon could not begrudge him one single moment of that happiness. Andy had earned it with years of dedication and hard work serving the same people Simon was trying to help now.

Of course Andy had wished him well for his presentation on the pilot study they had worked so hard together to make reality. He believed that Kate O'Neill would be an ideal replacement for him at the conference, and well able to back Simon up in the technical questions.

What Andy did not know—and what he could never know because Simon had not told him—was that Simon and Kate had a history together. Andy had been replaced by the only woman who had every reason to hate his guts. The same woman he needed to be his most avid supporter.

Just fantastic!

Simon ran one hand through his hair, which was freshly coated with a layer of dry red dust from the long road trip from the village. They were late—he was late—and the village of several hundred people had placed its economic future in his hands. He could not let them down—he *would* not let them down.

He needed a shower and to change, and most of all he needed to persuade Kate O'Neill to take him seriously before the media circus arrived and the pressure really started.

Of course this was only about the work.

The lump in his throat and the thumping of blood in his head had nothing at all to do with the fact that in three years his Katie had grown into the beautiful woman he had always known she would become. Only this time he needed her to be the best friend he had in this world.

That meant she would have to put aside the fact that after three years at university together, where they had shared their lives, dreams and hopes and every waking moment, he had dumped her only days after they'd graduated.

Apart from that...

Time to get to work. He could only pray that she was ready to do the same.

Simon sighed out loud and sniffed.

He was doomed.

Kate stood on the terrace looking out towards the ocean, with her fingers clasped hard around the smooth wooden rail, willing herself to be steady, resolute and professional and failing on every count.

She had never expected the sight of Simon Reynolds to destroy her composure like this, but it had—in every way possible. And it had nothing to do with the past few exhausting days and everything to do with how much she still felt about this man.

Which made her so angry she clenched her nails even harder into the wooden railing.

He had been the one who had walked out on her.

He had been the one who had been full of promises and not kept one of them.

He had been… He had been the love of her life, who had left her behind just like all the other men in her life who had abandoned her when the going got tough. If it had not been for her stepfather, Tom, she would have given up on the whole sorry lot of them a long time ago. Now Simon was here, in this stunning country, and she was going to have to deal with him.

A peal of happy children's laughter rang out from the beach below, interrupting her thoughts, and Kate blinked hard in the dazzling bright morning light to focus on the stunning view before her.

The hotel terrace faced the ocean, and the beautifully kept lawns stretched out to a wide strip of glowing white sand, where her view of the lapping waves was broken only by the thin trunks of tall palm trees.

It was like a poster of a dream beach from the cover of a holiday brochure, complete with a long wooden canoe on the shore and umbrellas made from palm fronds to protect the professional sunbathers from the heat of the African sun in January.

Palm trees. She was looking at real African coconut palm trees. The sky was a cloudless bright blue, and the warm breeze was luxuriously dry and scented with the salty tang from the sea blended with spice and a tropical sweet floral scent.

A great garland of bougainvillea with stunning bright purple and hot pink flowers wound its way around the handrail, intertwined with a wonderful frangipani which spilled out from a blue ceramic pot, attracting nectar-seeking insects to the intensely fragrant blossoms.

Kate spent most of her life in small air-conditioned computer rooms surrounded by office equipment and machinery. It was only natural that she should bend down to appreciate the frangipani flowers close up. Only the biggest insect she had ever seen in her life was inside one of the flowers at the time, and decided to leave just as she bent her head to sniff the blossom. Insect and cheek collided, and the insect was just as unhappy about that fact as she was.

Ouch! 'Oh, no, you don't,' Kate mumbled as she stood up and wafted the offending creature away. 'No wasp stings. Not on my first morning in Africa.'

'Hello, Katie,' came a voice as familiar as her own. 'Talking to yourself again?'

CHAPTER TWO

'WELL, this is quite a surprise,' Simon said, in that educated formal voice which could only come from a lifetime of privilege and expensive private schools. And it was still as amazingly, jaw-droppingly able to light a match under her fire more than any other voice she had ever known.

Her heart and body leapt to attention at the sound of his voice, so fast and so loudly she was surprised that he had not heard it. Speech was impossible, and it maddened her more than she could say that he still had the power to unsettle her so badly.

But she was determined not to let him see that he had got to her. Those days were long gone.

'Hi, Simon,' she said through a dry throat, in as casual and controlled a voice as she could imagine. 'Likewise. I had no idea that you were still in Ghana.'

'Oh, yes,' he answered. 'Still here, still working, still unpaid and still a volunteer. I'm even in the same village. Unlike some people I could mention. It seems like *you* have come up in the world, Katie.' He tilted his head to one side and grinned. 'Congratulations. The company must have a lot of faith in you to suggest you take over from Andy at such short notice. That is quite an achievement.'

Simon pushed one hand deep into his trouser pocket as he leant his other elbow on the railing and towered over her, blocking the blazing sunlight from blinding her, but also shading her with his shadow.

To her unending shame Kate felt her neck flame red in embarrassment and delight that Simon should take pleasure in her promotion—or was it just the impact of that killer grin of white teeth against his unshaven deeply tanned skin?

'Thank you,' she whispered, 'although I certainly hadn't planned to be here. Yesterday morning I was in Mexico, expecting to fly home to a grey London for the weekend. Instead of which...' Kate waved her right hand in the air towards the rolling waves under the azure blue sky. 'Andy Parsons' little boys arrived ahead of schedule, so the company asked me to take his place for a few weeks.'

And then she paused, lifted her head, and looked deep into Simon's face. They were standing so close together that none of the other delegates who had ambled onto the wide long terrace around them could possibly hear what they were saying.

But that did not change the fact that their history together was real, and as far as she was concerned not as much in the past as she had imagined. The only way was to go forward and face the consequences.

'I hope my being here is not going to be a problem for you?'

Simon paused for a second, before turning slightly away from the rail so that his whole body was facing towards her. It was just the two of them on that part of the terrace.

And in those few seconds of silence every one of her senses was attuned to every tiny movement he made.

The way his once soft hands and arms had filled out to become sinewy, strong and powerful. The way the hairs on the back of his hands had been bleached almost blond by the sun, which made them stand out pale and golden against the deep brown tan. And the way his pale grey eyes widened and then narrowed as he looked away from the ocean and back to her. The crease marks at the corners of his eyes were paler than the rest of the tan that if anything made him even more handsome than before—if that was possible.

He had always been able to mesmerise her with just a look.

And then his gaze hardened, and with one look straight into her eyes Simon answered her question without having to say a word.

The surface might have changed, but on the inside he was exactly the same man who had walked away from her and the chaos he'd left behind on that hot July morning three years ago—and he had not forgiven her for choosing to stay with her family instead of coming out to Africa with him, just as she had not forgiven him for leaving. One. Little. Bit.

'It's wonderful news about Andy. But does that mean you're taking his place just for the conference or as project manager for all the local IT initiatives?' Simon asked in a low, calm, steady voice—his serious voice, with a tiny lift of concern at the end.

'Both,' she replied with a slight nod. 'I'll be covering the conference, then shadowing Molly on a field visit to Andy's two new projects along the coast. In the meantime I need to catch up with the progress reports. According to Molly, Andy was supervising the project you are working on. I suppose that means that I'll be your acting project supervisor for the next few weeks.'

She gulped down her apprehension and disquiet.

'I need to know whether we can work together, Simon,' she said quickly, but Simon was already ahead of her, and he shook his head slowly as his grey eyes bored into hers.

'Don't worry about me, Katie. I can work with you any time. The real question is are you willing to work with me? I need to know that I can rely on you completely over the next few days. Especially during the press conferences and TV interviews.'

Kate felt her blood rise, and her fingers clutched even tighter into the handrail until she feared that she would have no nails left.

'What do you mean, TV interviews? That wasn't on the agenda I saw,' she replied, bristling with indignation at his implied accusation that she was not capable of doing the job as well as Andy could.

Simon raised both hands in the air in submission. 'I don't mean to criticise. It is just that there is a lot at stake here, and I really need to bring you up to date with my project as Andy's replacement. Whatever happens, we are going to have to work together as a team.'

'Then I suggest you start talking.' Kate picked up her dossier and waved it at Simon, still bristling at his implied concern. 'Which areas of the report do you expect to be asked questions on?'

Simon nodded. 'I have known Andy so long he probably didn't record the details, but the local tribal leaders in my village have invited me to do something pretty special, and Andy was going to use it as part of the PR plan to help with extra fundraising for the project.'

Kate looked from the report back to Simon in confusion, her throat dry.

'Okay,' she replied in a quivering voice, trying to sound confident and not in the least upset that all the plans she had carefully sketched out for her day had probably just been blown away. 'Can you tell me about it now?'

Before Simon could answer there was a great cacophony of loud car horns mixed with angry shouting and lively chatter coming from the road leading up to the hotel. Both Simon and Kate leant out over the terrace railing just in time to see a huge white TV camera van drive across the pristine lawns to overtake two large off-road estate cars which had tried to squeeze through the narrow road at the same time. They had crashed into one another and were now blocking the entrance to the hotel

'Too late. Sorry, Katie, I'll have to tell you all about it later. I need to find a shower and get changed before the media frenzy gets underway.'

Kate threw up her hands and pointed to his chest, blocking him from running back inside.

'Frenzy! Simon Reynolds, you are not moving from this terrace until I know what is going on. What is it that you are not telling me?'

'Oh. Right. Yes. A few weeks ago the principal King of my village invited me to become their Chief of Development—the Ngoryi-Fia—which means that I am now officially a royal prince of the tribal kingdom I call home. It is an amazing honour.' Simon took one glance at Kate's shocked face and smiled. 'My coronation is next Saturday, if you're still around. It could be your only chance to see a geek being crowned as King.'

'Prince? Royal? King?' Kate squawked, and Simon grinned at her and shrugged his shoulders as she pressed one hand to her chest in shock.

'I know that it is hard to take in. I'm still getting used to the idea myself. We only have one royal family in Britain, while in Ghana…?' He raised his hands in the air. 'It is a *very* different story.'

'But…how? I mean, when did all this happen?' Kate spluttered, her head still spinning.

'A few weeks ago. I only hope the press pick up the real story, about how much the community suffered when the cocoa business failed. The whole region needs as much sponsorship as we can get. Your company has done a brilliant job with the pilot scheme I am running, but there are a dozen villages where they need the same support.'

'Sponsors, story, prince,' Kate murmured, and shook her head. 'Any more shocks you would like to spring on me? Just to get them all out of the way at once, as it were?'

Simon frowned and pretended to think. 'No, I don't think there is anything else at the moment. But I wasn't joking about having to put on a united front for the media. Andy wanted to make sure that the press knew that your company were still going to fund the next phase of the pilot study. Sort of a win/win for both of us. That was the plan. If you are up for it?'

She scowled at him. 'Oh, I am up for it. If we need to create a united front for the media then I'll see it through.'

Then she smiled and waved at a group of hotel guests who had wandered onto the terrace. 'Just as long as you don't expect me to bow and scrape and call you Prince Simon!' she hissed under her breath.

'Not at all. We are old friends, after all,' he replied without a hint of sarcasm. 'And you know the sacrifices we made to make this happen.'

Kate lifted her chin. At last he had said something she could relate to.

'Oh, I never had any doubt that you would get the job done. You made it abundantly clear that was the only thing that you were interested in when you left.'

Simon turned and focused his laser-sharp gaze on her face as she continued to smile at the other people behind his back. His voice was just low enough to make sure that his calm words were for her alone.

'You know that my father made commitments and promises to the people and the villages. He promised that he would not let them down, and I wasn't prepared to let all that work go to waste. It was my job to continue the work he had started and make good those promises. And that is what I've been doing this last three years, Katie. Building on what he started.'

'Terrific. Then I look forward to hearing your presentation this afternoon.'

The air was fierce between them, crackling with energy and emotion, and the feeling was so intense that Kate was almost grateful when the new arrival of delegates burst through onto the terrace, filling the space with lively chatter and energy and bringing her down to earth with a smash.

She glanced at her watch, then peeked inside the lounge, which was starting to fill up.

'You'll have to excuse me. I need to go through the project timelines before the conference presentation starts.'

A shadow of a smile flashed across Simon's mouth so fast that anyone else would have missed it. Strange how she remembered that little twitch at the side of his mouth so well. It was like an old friend saying hello.

'Of course. I was hoping to report back to the tribal elders tonight about how the press events went, so it would be nice to make a start—*Miss O'Neill.*'

It was the first time he had used her surname. And the way he threw it down to her like a gauntlet across the face shocked her more than she wanted to admit. Three years ago she had been forced to choose between keeping her own promises and helping Simon keep the promises his dead father had made. Now he was getting his own back. And she was going to have to take it because, like it or not, it looked as if Simon Reynolds was her project leader, and her promotion depended on her ability to work with him. One to one.

'Then I suggest we get started, *Mr Reynolds.* Shall we say thirty minutes in the main conference room?'

'Looking forward to it,' he said, his eyes sparkling with something close to wicked humour. 'See you in thirty minutes. *Partner.*'

CHAPTER THREE

WITH a low groan, Kate propped her elbows on the table, dropped her head into her hands and pressed her fingers onto her throbbing temples.

She was pathetic.

'Are you feeling okay, Kate?' Molly asked, her gentle voice full of concern as she softly touched Kate's arm.

I am surrounded by kind people who are here to help me do a great job, Kate thought. *I am an idiot.*

Kate immediately sat back and smiled. Time to snap out of this and get the work done. Molly had a conference to keep on track.

'Touch of a headache. Nothing to worry about,' she replied, and watched Molly's frown relax. 'I'm fine. Do you need me to help you with anything?

Molly shook her head. 'The other way round. I've tracked down this fine young man, who has been working with Simon on one of the projects you have just taken over. He has a few minutes to spare, so this is a good time to get to know each other before the presentations start.'

Molly turned to one side and gestured towards a tall, gangly teenager who had been lurking behind her. 'Paul, this is Kate O'Neill, who I was telling you about. I'm sure she would love to hear about the programme in your village. Why don't you sit down and join her?'

Kate grinned and held out her hand towards Paul, who reached out his long arm and gave her fingers a brief shake before sitting down awkwardly opposite her. Before Molly could join them the reception desk filled up again, and Molly excused herself and took off.

'Lovely to meet you, Paul,' Kate said, as she took in Paul's immaculately pressed white long-sleeved shirt, smart black trousers with a sharp crease, and black briefcase.

He was tall, and his shoulders and chest were just filling out, so she was guessing that he was probably around sixteen or seventeen years old, yet there was a certain air of confidence about him which blended with a certain touch of childlike wonder that was absolutely charming. This one was going to break hearts one day.

Paul, on the other hand, seemed totally uninterested in her, and was staring, apparently mesmerised, at the laptop computer she had in front of her, at her palm-top organiser on the table next to it, and her smartphone. All the latest models from top suppliers.

Men. Kate chuckled to herself.

Once the way to a man's heart had been through his stomach. Now it was through whatever the latest gadget or gizmo the world had created—especially at technology conferences.

'I would love to catch up with some of Andy's projects, Paul. I did not have time to go through the field reports before flying out here, so anything you can tell me would be a great help.'

Paul dragged his gaze away from the technology and gave her a dazzling smile. Oh, yes, the girls would be queuing for miles to have that smile turned on them. No doubt at all. Heartbreaker in the making.

'Of course, Miss O'Neill. I would be very pleased to

answer any of your questions,' Paul replied, in English so perfect that she could cut it with a knife. Which totally stunned her for a second. Either Paul had been in expensive formal education in Britain, or somewhere in Ghana there was an impressive coaching service for spoken English.

Kate swallowed down her personal prejudices. She had worked hard to learn how to speak correctly and cover up the strong regional dialect and poor speech patterns from her early years. She had no right at all to judge someone whose parents had probably worked just as hard to afford an education for their son. Even if it did rattle her a little.

After all, wasn't his voice one of the many things which had attracted her to Simon Reynolds on that first day at university? She'd yearned to be around people who had been brought up to speak that way from the day they were born. Be part of that crowd. Overcome what she had left behind in her old life and reinvent herself as a new person.

That was why she had agreed to move with Tom and Gemma to the historic university town, with its ancient stone walls and centuries of history. So that she could start all over again.

She had taken her adopted father's surname instead of her real name, and matched it to a new voice, new haircut and clothes. New hopes and aspirations. New dreams.

Kate swallowed hard and pushed down the instinctive urge to copy Paul's speech patterns. He might think that she was mocking him, the way she'd used to copy Simon and make him laugh so hard he fell off his chair. And that would not be fair to Paul.

Especially when all he was here for was the conference, which must look like Santa's grotto to any teenager not used to being surrounded by the latest technology.

'Here's an idea. Why don't you start by describing the communication systems you are using at the moment? Do you have a satellite phone and laptops? And what comms software are you running?'

Paul's bright eyes widened, and a cheeky grin picked up the corners of his mouth when he answered. 'It would help if I could take a look at *your* computer. Just to compare.'

'Really?' Kate nodded, and pretended to consider. 'Well, in that case, please feel free to fiddle as much as you like.'

With that she gave a short laugh, and turned the notebook computer around so that Paul could see it. Kate looked on in delight as Paul wiggled his shoulders and fingers a little, as though preparing to present some amazing magic trick. He had just lifted the lid and powered it up when Simon stepped out of the elevator, tugged once on the cuff of each jacket sleeve, and lifted his chin with a smile. She was smitten. Seriously, jelly legs smitten.

He had changed into a charcoal-grey business suit with a pale blue shirt and a striped blue and pink-banded narrow tie. The crisp shirt collar contrasted with the deep tan of his face and neck, and the sun-bleached tips of his clean, swept-back hair. Shiny black shoes. Smart watch.

Despite the business suit, the preppy version of the Simon she'd used to know was gone. Now there was a shocking air of wildness about him which seemed to call out to her. His dark curly hair was cropped short to match his sharply chiselled features, and he had lost weight but gained muscle. Under the smart clothing Simon Reynolds looked like a man who worked outdoors every day instead of running a computer server.

And there was something else. The way he held his head, his stance, his body language and even the low pitch of his voice screamed out confidence and power. He had done well here. Two of the other men even gave him a gentle bow of respect as they came up to him and bent their heads over the agenda for the day.

Suddenly she was a student again, on her first day at university. Terrified. Exhilarated. Excited and totally, totally intimidated by the clever rich people who surrounded her.

Looking back, she felt sorry for that girl who had been so crippled by her own feelings of insecurity and her lack of self-worth, and the deep-held belief that she did not even deserve to be there, at that prestigious university where really clever and important people went to learn.

Only there'd been this boy at the back of the class, talking about computers and technology, and his voice had been so confident and rich and embracing that she hadn't been able to stop herself being drawn across the threshold and into the new and incredible world she had longed to be part of.

Simon had been holding court as though he was the lecturer, and as he'd lifted his head he had winked at her. Her world had shifted and she'd known that she was doomed. One simple gesture was all it took. She'd been eighteen going on nineteen on the surface, but about fourteen on the inside, just melting with the heat and boiling turmoil that one look created.

He'd made her feel as though she was starting out fresh all over again.

Simon Reynolds had been the golden boy of the class. His father had been a famous IT guru who was about to launch another company after selling his dotcom start-up for millions. There had even been a profile of him in the Sunday newspapers.

Simon had been so far out of her league he'd been playing in a different game where she'd had no idea of the rules. When he'd asked her out the first time she had actually thought it was some sort of cruel joke, and laughed it off as just that. When he'd asked her the second time she'd started to get interested.

He must have asked her out several times each month before she'd finally relented over coffee and a seminar they were both taking, when one of the lecturers had thought it would be interesting to pair them up on a project.

Dynamite. Explosive, competitive and intellectual dynamite.

She'd had no idea how much fun it could be to spar with someone who was just as clever as she was and just as quick—but Simon had been funny with it. She'd been geek girl, only interested in being top of her class and the pot of gold at the end of the rainbow in the form of a top-paying job. He'd been the golden boy who could do no wrong, who didn't need the money but who loved the challenge.

How could she not have fallen for him? How could she not have been totally in awe of the great Simon Reynolds? And when she'd got to know him better… Ah, that was when she'd slipped into love without even realising it.

But that had been long years ago, and they were both different people now.

Nevertheless it was a struggle to smile gently as Simon strolled over to them and dropped his arm onto Paul's shoulder just long enough to give him a reassuring shake.

'I see you two have met. Excellent. I can always rely on Paul to seek out the latest technology and the prettiest girls.'

Kate's lips curled. She was not going to be drawn into that one, even if Paul *was* looking up at Simon with nothing less than adulation. There was a genuine friendship here, and she envied them that. But she could not dwell on missed opportunities. It was time to clear the air so that they could move forward—and if Simon could look at it that way then so could she, no matter how much it hurt.

'Hi, Simon,' she said with a smile. 'Nice suit. But you really shouldn't have gone to all that trouble just for me.'

Her reward was a lopsided hidden smile. The left side of his mouth twisted up and his eyes crinkled to match, just enough to show that he knew exactly what she was up to.

'Oh, this old thing,' he replied, and pretended to straighten his tie. 'Had it for years. Thought I would give it a bit of an outing. Don't want to let the village or the company down.'

Then he paused, and she could feel the intensity of his eyes as they flicked down her body from head to toe, making her squirm and blush—which was clearly his intention. 'Good to know that you still choose grey too. That must be very reassuring. To know that you always have the same colour hanging in your wardrobe.'

The silence stretched out between them, his grey eyes burning into hers. And they both knew that he was not talking about clothing.

He was thinking of people like his dad, who spent their entire working lives in offices wearing the same kind of suit as every other man in the office. Even his dad had traded in his jeans and T-shirts for the corporate look, but he had laughed it off with talk about putting on a costume so that he could play a part, like some actor in a movie where *he* had written the script. It had been a game, an act. At least for a while.

Perhaps Simon had changed? If he was prepared to put on a business suit for the sake of the people he was helping, then he might just be someone she could learn to trust. Again.

'Actually, this is the *only* suit hanging in my wardrobe.

My luggage did not catch the same flight,' she replied with a rueful smile. 'So you might be seeing this suit for a few more days to come.'

Simon laughed out loud, and then quickly scanned the foyer before closing the gap between them, holding his paperwork as though they were talking business. Only Kate noticed the tell-tale way that he licked his bottom lip and paused for a fraction of a second before he looked into her face and said, 'Best of luck with that. But…um…do you have a few minutes to spare? There are a couple of things we need to go through before the sessions open. I'm sure Paul will look after your laptop while you are away.'

Simon held open the door and watched Kate stroll in her high heels across the sunlit foyer into one of the small boardrooms. Everything told him to call after her with some vague excuse when her steps slowed and she half turned and looked back at him over one shoulder. He fell into her blue eyes and was a teenager again, lost and bewildered around this girl he had never been truly able to fathom but who challenged him and attracted him like no other girl before or since.

If she had been an enigma to him then, the elegant and professional grown-up version of Kate he was looking at now was a miracle sent back into his life at just the worst time possible. Or was it the best?

The fact that she was here for the company who were sponsoring his eco-technology project was a matter of fact, too hard to be avoided.

'What is it, Simon?' she asked quietly across the space and the years that separated them, and he could hear the strain in her soft voice. Her cheeks were flushed despite the air-conditioning, her blue eyes wide and sad and imploring.

And he was right back to seeing her for the first time all over again.

How did she do it?

He had spent the last three years fighting to get over her and convince himself that he had made the right decision to come to Ghana and leave her behind!

He had a job he was obsessed about, responsibilities for people who were relying on him for their future, and enough worries to last him a lifetime—and here she was, waltzing into his life out of the blue and destroying any hope he had of getting through this next week with something like control.

She knew him. There had been a time when she'd known him better than his parents ever could. Shared his dreams and hopes and fears. Until fate stepped in and ripped them apart.

No. He had to get it together for the people who needed him now. *Today.*

It was time to prove to his village that they had made the right decision when they'd made him Prince and asked him to be their King.

Katie was here from the company who made his work possible. He needed her to be on his side all the way. The rest of the day was going to be a blur of business and media events. If he was going to do it at all, then he had to do it now.

He could only hope that she was willing to accept an apology from the man who had hurt her.

'This isn't about work, Katie,' he said with his arms crossed, and then he uncrossed them. 'Well, it is—but not directly. I've been thinking about what you said this morning, and we really do need to sort things out if we are going to be working together.'

'Oh? I thought you said everything that needed to be

said the last time we met. You were certainly clear enough
then that you never wanted to see me again, unless I was
prepared to leave my dad and Gemma behind and come
out here with you,' Katie said, and turned away from him
with a sigh that pierced his heart.

'I know,' he whispered. A lump the size of Wales had
formed in Simon's throat, and he did not dare to speak. He
leant his hands on the back of the nearest chair instead,
and watched her pause and turn back to face him, confusion creasing her brow.

'You know?' Kate bit her lower lip the way she'd used
to when she was nervous.

In a way that simple gesture reassured him that the old
Katie was still in there, beneath the professional grey skirt
suit and the discreet jewellery and straight long blonde
hair. He had never seen hair that colour anywhere. Ash
blonde mixed with something. It had always fallen long
and straight and he had never understood why she hated
it. She had no idea how stunning she looked. To her it was
a dumb blonde look that was going to ruin her chances of
being taken seriously in business. He had even stopped her
from dying it dark brown once. How could he ever tire of
running his fingers through that long silky blonde hair,
smoothing it down over and over again?

He cursed himself for missing out on the time that they
could have spent together.

'I still cringe when I think about how cruel I was. I am
so sorry for leaving you when your dad was sick. I should
have been strong enough to stay and work it out, but I just
couldn't. And I am so very sorry. I regret leaving you like
that more than I can say.'

CHAPTER FOUR

'YOU'RE sorry?' Kate looked at him with amazement and something close to bewilderment in the depths of her wide, sad blue eyes.

'After my father died…we were all such a mess that it was hard to think straight…'

Kate dropped her head for a moment, and Simon's heart sank to the pit of his stomach at the thought that he was hurting her.

Her head lifted, but she paused just long enough to tell him that this time she was not going to avoid the massive elephant in the room. 'You didn't want to talk about what happened between my dad and your mum, and I understood that because neither did I. But running away with you would have meant leaving my dad and Gemma behind just when they needed me most.'

'What happened between them? Let's be honest, Katie. They had been sleeping together for months. I would call that an affair. Wouldn't you? Because that was certainly how my dad described it. Oh—about two hours before he drove his car into a tree and killed himself.'

'You don't think I remember that? We were together when the police knocked on the door. I went with you to where the accident happened and saw what was left of the car. The investigators said he just lost control, Simon. Why can't you accept that?'

The words swirled around inside Simon's head and he squeezed his eyes tight shut against the blinding heat of the sun as it broke through the window.

Just lost control.

Kate moved closer but clenched her right hand, steadying herself for what was coming next.

He knew that he did not have to explain those images to Kate. He did not have to because she had shared every one of them.

It was Kate who had taken his hand and stood by his side every step on that day, until she was too exhausted to go on.

Kate who had slept on the sofa so that she could be with him.

Kate who had tried to balance out the overwhelming despair which had turned to anger over the next few horrific days.

Kate who had tried to make him understand that his mother needed him.

Kate who had taken the brunt of all of his rage against the mother he loved so much but who in his eyes had betrayed his father and caused his death, who he could not bring himself to speak to face to face.

Kate who had held him when he cried.

Kate who told him that he could get through this.

And Kate who had had the power to destroy him when she'd refused to go with him. She had been his only friend, his best friend. And more.

'You made me choose between staying with my family and being with you. It was hard, Simon. So very hard. And you need to know that if it hadn't been for Gemma I would

have packed my rucksack, taken your hand and walked
away from all that chaos. And, believe me, I wanted to do
that just as much as you did.'

Her voice quivered with the intensity of her feelings,
and it was all there in her eyes for him to see.

She was telling him the truth. After all these years.
And, whether it was absolution or regret that he was feeling, Simon felt as though a spring that had been held tight
inside his heart had suddenly uncoiled.

'You wanted to go with me?'

She nodded. 'I followed you to the end of the road,' she
whispered. 'And hid in the neighbour's garden until you
turned the corner and were out of sight. It would have been
so easy to run after you and just go. My passport was in
my pocket. I had saved a little money in the bank. Yes. Of
course I wanted to go with you. But…'

There was a deep sadness in those blue eyes which
reached out and touched him at the very spot where a big
black hole called Katie had used to live, and the tiny pilot
light he had persuaded himself had been put out burst into
action. A gentle orange flame flickered into life, warm and
welcome and as unsettling as a forest fire.

So he had not imagined it after all. Their relationship
had meant as much to her as it had to him.

Simon shuffled two steps closer to her, his eyes fixed
on the table where they were standing. Anywhere but on
her face. Her face would be too much.

'Were you scared?' he asked, in a low voice.

Her answer was a whisper. 'Not for myself. I had sur-
vived a lot more than you knew to earn that place at university. I would have got by. But you hadn't lived that life,
Simon. You had grown up with more than enough money
to do whatever and go wherever you wanted, and your parents were always there for you. Then suddenly your father

was gone and you wouldn't even talk to your mother. I was scared for you and what you were going to have to face alone out here. I was frightened for you. But I knew that I had to let you go. And that was so hard.'

'Is that why you told me that you loved me?' he asked. 'To try and persuade me to change my mind about going? Or did you mean it?'

Kate's fingers pressed against the back of his hand for a fleeting second, and she opened her mouth to answer— but before she could say the words there was a bustle of activity and lively chatter at the door to the boardroom, and Molly popped her head around the door with a broad grin.

'Ah. There you are, Simon. The TV crew will be ready for you in a few minutes. Sorry to interrupt, Kate, but the star of the conference needs to make his first royal speech. See you in a few minutes.' And with a small finger-wave she pulled the door closed.

Simon and Kate looked at each other for a few seconds before she took the initiative, reached out and straightened his tie.

'Looks like it's time to get out there and meet your public, Your Majesty. Your subjects await.' With one final shake of the head Kate smiled warmly at him and said in a low, soft voice which thrilled him beyond belief, 'Let's go and tell them what you've been up to these last three years. *Partner.*'

Two hours later Kate collapsed down onto a hard chair in the huge ballroom which served as the main conference area and slipped off her shoes, rubbing her poor crushed toes back to life.

Frenzy had been just about right. As soon as Simon appeared he had practically been mobbed by three teams of

TV reporters, all clamouring for interviews and the inside story on what it felt like to be the very first western Prince, soon to be King, of a tribal kingdom in rural Africa.

He had handled every one of the often daft questions about protocol and the best way to wear a toga with courtesy and style, while she and Molly had run themselves ragged handing out press releases and project reports on the company's IT products and the current sponsorship programme in this part of Africa. It had almost been a relief that most of the questions had been aimed at the star of the day—all she'd had to do was stand next to Simon with Molly for the compulsory photo call.

When his arm had snaked behind her back, pressing her close to his side, her smile had become even more fixed and professional. No speaking part required, thank goodness.

Now the media crews had drifted into the dining room like locusts, for the free buffet lunch the company had provided, giving her a precious few moments to catch her breath before the official conference welcome session.

Shame that she was already exhausted and the real work had not even started. *Whimper.*

What made it even worse was that Simon seemed as fresh as ever. She could only watch in awe as he ran through his talk with Paul.

'You are going to be just fine,' Simon said, and pointed at the projection screen behind Paul's head. 'The presentation looks great. One more run-through and we're done. Okay? Okay.' With one final nod Simon strolled to the back of the room, sat down next to her, and stretched out his long legs before pointing towards the podium where Paul was fiddling with the laptop.

'I hope you don't mind but I've asked Paul to give the presentation on the pilot study. I think it will mean a lot more if it comes from one of the pupils instead of the project worker who started it.'

'Actually, I think that's a great idea—especially when Paul is so eloquent. Is he your star pupil?'

The smile on Simon's face widened into grin of delight and pleasure, which startled Kate. The affection and delight he obviously felt for this boy was genuine.

'Paul is the son of the paramount King of our area, and probably the greatest natural talent I've ever seen. You would never believe that he only touched his first personal computer at the age of twelve. He is already head boy of the local school, and I think he's a genius. The only thing holding that boy back is the lack of opportunity and equipment. This is where we come in.'

Katie tilted her head slightly to one side. 'I think there is more to it than that. Do you want to tell me about it?'

Simon shook his head before replying. 'You could always see right through me, couldn't you? And you're right. Paul's father gave me a home when I needed one, took me in, and then listened to my crazy schemes to introduce solar power and digital technology to a village which at that time had only the most basic school building. And by basic I mean no educational materials at all. No books and certainly no money to pay for teachers. They were doing the best they could, but it was tough.'

Kate nodded then pursed her lips. 'Sorry to question your ability, Your Royal Highness, but I can't see you as a junior school teacher.'

Simon chuckled. 'I tried, but there are people better qualified to teach the basics these children need before they can even use a computer. I learned pretty fast that food and clean water and a safe place to sleep are higher up the priority list than a reliable internet connection.'

Kate sighed out loud. 'Do you remember the first time

you dragged me to that talk on graduate volunteer projects in Africa? I blame you entirely for my whole career.'

He snorted out a reply. 'You used to call it my middle class obsession. I certainly didn't expect that we would both be working in the same field all these years later. Perhaps it is just as well that we can never truly know how things are going to turn out? Although…'

'Although?' Kate asked, half turning in her chair so that she could face him.

'Don't hit me, but I was surprised when Andy told me that you had already worked on projects in India and Mexico. After what happened with Dad, I did wonder…' Simon raised both eyebrows and gave her a gentle closed-mouth smile.

'You thought I might stay clear of volunteer work?' Kate said with a lilt in her voice. 'That's a fair question, and the truth is, yes, I *did* think very long and hard about working overseas. But at the end of the day this is the fastest way to step up the promotion ladder to head office.'

Simon nodded. 'Which means you could live at home? Right. That makes sense.' He turned away from her, as though disappointed.

'Wait a minute, Simon. Don't get me wrong. I wouldn't be doing this unless I believed that the work was important. And it *is* important. That is what this conference is all about—and I never, ever confused the work you were doing with why you left.'

She leant forward and locked onto his grey eyes.

'Perhaps it's time to show me what you have been up to these past three years before I read it in Andy's report? Let's get this conference started.'

CHAPTER FIVE

KATE stood sideways to check her profile in the mirror and immediately pulled in her stomach, vowing that, no matter where she went, from this minute onwards she would always pack a jersey dress or something—*anything*—that would fold up small and not crease in her hand luggage instead of her suitcase.

It was no good. Whatever she did there was no way that the dress she had borrowed from Molly Evans was going to hide the bulges that came from several years' worth of snatched meals and sitting hunched over a computer terminal for twelve hours every day of the week.

Molly was a lovely lady, and had been very generous to offer her the use of a dress for the conference dinner. The grey business suit was fine for daywear, but people were bound to notice if she was to wear it again for the dinner that evening, and then all the next day—even longer if her missing suitcase did not turn up.

She turned quickly from side to side with her arms outstretched, and watched in relief as the silky fabric of the maxi-dress slid loosely over her hips.

That only left one problem area.

Kate tugged at the side of the dress and tried to hitch it up a little further, but her generous bosom had already filled all the spare fabric. Worse, an enormous shell-pink passion flower now covered her left breast, creating a very different type of eye-catching design.

Options… *Come on, Kate,* she told herself. *Time to get creative! That's what they pay you for.*

Kate flung open the wardrobe door and gazed at the meagre contents of the rails. She blinked several times at the pathetic range of lingerie she always carried in her hand luggage, right to left and back again, pulled each item out and held it against the dress—and instantly noticed how the shell-pink of her fitted pyjama top matched the shade of pink in the dress almost exactly.

The pyjama jacket might just work as a make-do bolero top. *It just might.*

Even if she was going to be in the presence of dignitaries and royalty. Including several princes. And one in particular.

Kate's left hand pressed hard against the wardrobe to support her weight.

Simon was Prince of a Ghanaian village and was going to be crowned King in a few days.

Her Simon. A king. *A king!*

That afternoon she had sat in the front row of the conference room as Paul talked through slide after slide of stunning colour pictures of the village where he had been born and had spent his life, and the amazing countryside which surrounded it. Dazzling photographs of wide tranquil lakes covered with water lilies had been followed by shots of thick jungle forest land, backed up by cliffs with spectacular cascading waterfalls.

It looked a magical and awe-inspiring place, made real by the people Paul and Simon shared their lives with.

To her eyes Simon had dominated every scene, whether he was carrying bricks for the half-built tiny schoolroom, or balancing on a couple of rusty oil drums to repair a leaking roof in the middle of a tropical downpour. It was Simon who had leapt out at her from the photos of tribal leaders in their ceremonial robes, coming together to celebrate the opening of the first solar energy unit. His pride of being part of their community had shone out.

The presentation had been a revelation, and had earned both Paul and Simon a standing ovation from the entire conference.

Wow. Something that felt an awful lot like pride welled up inside her, and she blinked away the prick of tears in the corner of her eyes. Allergies. *Must be her allergies.*

Of course he had always been the golden boy, expected to take over his father's company when he left university. Shame that his family had had no idea that the business had serious financial problems—how could they? His father had not told them about the trouble he was in—not even when he was flying all over Africa investigating alternative technology initiatives.

Sometimes she'd used to wonder how things would have turned out for them if Simon's father had not become so obsessed with this amazing country. But she had played the 'what-if' game too many times and the result was always the same—his father was dead and it was too late to turn back the clock. She and Simon had been student lovers, that was all—happened all the time. You met someone at college and then you had to grow up and go out and live your life.

But with Simon it was different.

This time Simon was going to be a king—not because of some inheritance, but because he had earned that honour through his own investment and hard work. His father might have sparked the original idea for a digital communication centre, but it was Simon who had made that dream a reality by his own sweat and his constant drive to find sponsorship and support from any organisation or charity with the resources he needed.

There was no point in denying it. She *was* proud of him.

Kate pushed her arms into the sleeves of her pyjama top, took one final glance in the full-length mirror and twirled from side to side, then lifted her hair up into a loose twist.

Much better! In fact it was positively regal.

Time to shout about Simon's good news from the rooftops. Starting with one very special little lady. Her sister Gemma—who would want to know everything!

Simon pulled on a faded T-shirt bearing the name of a pop group nobody here would know, and peeked through the blind of his hotel room window. The sun was already low on the horizon, but this was the first time he had felt able to escape the bustling crowds and constant banter from reporters and other volunteers which had followed him all day. The conference had become a hotspot for anyone looking for a human interest story to fill a gap in a news report or magazine around the world—and today it was his turn to be in the spotlight.

He had been hijacked—and he had to put up with it. No matter how much he squirmed inside when the cameras were pointing at him. He was prepared to act out his part and do his bit. His village community and the project were all that mattered. Not him.

Molly had dug out an old photograph from the tribal meeting when he had first worn a toga and added it to the press release at the very last minute. Embarrassed did not come close!

Simon cringed at the mental picture of poor, unsuspecting readers opening their newspapers at breakfast tables and on tube trains on the way to work back in England and finding *that* horrific image staring back at them.

Of course Molly Evans had done a wonderful job in the PR department—that was her job—and Kate had backed him up every step of the way. But by the end of the formal presentations he had felt as though the village chiefs who had recognised his commitment to building their future and offered him this amazing honour had become lost in the rush to focus on him and *his* unique story instead of theirs.

He didn't blame the press for being interested—he would be too. But there were only so many times he could tell his personal story without making himself out to be some sort of hero. Which was so very far from the truth it was ridiculous.

If they only knew that he was the last person in the world he would have called a hero.

If they wanted to know what sacrifices he had made to be here then all they had to do was ask Kate O'Neill. The only person who truly knew every one of his many faults.

He had spent most of the day looking out of the corner of his eye for a glimpse of a blonde-haired girl in a grey suit.

And she had been everywhere—working, doing her job with elegance and panache!

Katie handing out conference goodie bags and notes from the four presentations that had followed the welcome session. Katie standing alongside Molly as they chatted to local government health department officials about the projects her company sponsored in Ghana. Katie introducing Paul to other charity organisations who had the resources they needed so desperately, giving him moral support when he faltered.

Katie. The girl who had been *his* Katie. Setting up meetings and printing out press releases and project proposals for the decision-makers. She probably hadn't realised that he was watching her, professional IT person in action, just as he had always imagined she would be. Intelligent, quick, dedicated and charming in her high-heeled executive shoes and smart grey suit. The company should be proud of what she'd achieved today.

He certainly was.

Simon closed his eyes and raked his fingers back through his hair.

Oh, Katie. As if his life was not in enough turmoil. The last thing he needed right now was Katie O'Neill turning up, just in time to stir up the past and take him back to a place where he had been so lost.

One thing was clear—he needed fresh air and to feel the wind on his face before he could brave a tight shirt collar, the stuffy conference dinner that evening, and all the extra media attention that would come with it.

The sun was an orange ball of stunning flame in a sky of the deepest azure blue with apricot streaks by the time Simon slipped down the stairs and out through a side door to the path leading to the shoreline.

He had always loved the sea. And so had Katie. The day after their second-year exams had finally been over he had shared a magical week away with Katie at a beach cottage in Dorset that his mother had rented from a friend for the whole of the summer. They had spent their days swimming and sunbathing, followed by barbecues and moonlit walks along the beach. And their nights…?

Simon stopped and closed his eyes for a second, reliving those heady nights of young love and the simple joy of waking up with Katie in his arms and a smile on his face. The sex and the intimacy had been so mind-bogglingly amazing they had changed his life.

He had never been happier.

Shaking his head with a contented grin, Simon waved

at the few hotel staff who were clearing away the debris left by their guests, and in the fading light stepped onto the white sand and strolled down the shore, away from the brightly lit hotel. Here the beach angled more sharply into the Atlantic, and the palms clung tightly to a narrow strip of shallow soil.

With every step he took further from the hotel Simon could feel the tension ease from his shoulders. Strange. He'd used to love the idea of working in high-tech offices surrounded by the buzz of electrical equipment and busy office chatter, the constant cacophony of telephones and fax machines and printers.

No longer. *This* was his idea of heaven.

The sound of waves from the Atlantic Ocean rolling pebbles onto the sandy beach only a few feet away. Sand beneath his feet. The trill and chirp of birdsong and the wind in the palm trees—all to the background noise of insect wings and frog calls. Somewhere a dog was barking and seagulls called. This was the soundtrack to his life and he loved it.

Simon dropped back his head, eyes closed, and just listened. Savouring the moment and trying to clear his head of the clutter and noise of the day.

That was probably why he felt like screaming out loud when the ring-tone from a cell phone destroyed his precious moment of calm. His eyes snapped open and he stomped across the beach for a few minutes to the shoreline, to where the sound had come from, intent on giving the owner his opinion.

But he didn't. *He couldn't.*

Because sitting on the shore, with her back pressed against a tree, was his Katie. She was alone and crying. And she seemed to be wearing a long, silky flowery nightdress and a pink pyjama top.

All his bluster and anger vanished in the breeze.

Her eyes were closed, but as he took a step closer his foot crunched down on a piece of driftwood and her eyelashes flicked several times as she reacted in alarm. Then they slowed and blinked away the trace of tears. One escaped and ran on to her cheek. She sniffed and quickly brushed it away with the back of her forefinger.

She tried to smile up at him, but her mouth didn't make it. Instead the fingers of both hands cupped tightly around the cell phone in her lap and she brought it up to her face in the fading light so that she could key in a few words of text.

He knelt down on the shoreline in front of her, with his back to the sun, and watched her read the message that came in reply to her text. A small smile creased her mouth before a single tear rolled down her cheek—only she had pressed her hand to her mouth so tightly that she could not wipe the tear away.

So Simon stretched out and moved the rough pad of his thumb across her soft cheek to do the job for her. Her delicate pale skin was illuminated against the ridges of his working hands. Her response was a sharp intake of breath and a wider smile—for him.

Neither of them spoke, but her eyes were locked on his now, and even when she dropped her phone onto her lap she did not look away.

What Simon saw in those eyes was something more than the look of a girl who had taken an upsetting phone call. It was a cry for help from someone who was not able or willing to say the words to ask for it.

And that look destroyed him.

He couldn't handle this as Prince Simon. For Katie he needed to go back to that first day at university, when he had managed to build up enough courage to actually speak to the prettiest girl in his year group instead of just winking at her and playing the idiot.

'Hi there, pretty girl. You new around here?'

And instantly, without hesitation or delay, she shot back with the same answer she had given him all those years ago—only this time in a croaky rather than jokey voice, 'Yes, but don't tell anyone. I'm supposed to be giving the lecture.'

And *then* the cool, collected, sophisticated businesswoman burst into tears.

CHAPTER SIX

IT SEEMED only right and natural for Simon to shuffle forward and take Kate into his arms, as he had done a hundred times before, and just like a familiar warm glove she slipped into the shape of his body as though she had never left. Her head fell onto his shoulder as she clung to him, her chest pressed against his, soaking in the strength and heat of his love and his support as he held her close.

As her sobs ebbed away Simon's hand moved in gentle wide circles around her lower back, just the way she'd used to like. He felt her chest heave with emotion, then slow to a more regular movement as her breathing calmed under his caresses.

His head pressed against her silky hair, but there was something sharp and hard under his chin and in the fading light he realised that she put her hair up. With two fingers he slowly pulled out the comb and two hair grips, and dropped them onto the beach towel she was sitting on. With exquisite pleasure the fingers of his right hand smoothed back the hair back from her forehead and gently, gently teased out the strands of her hair until it was falling in a waterfall of silken tresses over the back of his hand.

Kate shuffled slightly against him and he held his breath, in fear that she was going to break this tenuous, remarkable connection. But to his delight and wonder she was not moving away—she was snuggling closer. And his heart sang. He had never, ever expected to feel so powerfully like this again.

She felt so right. It was as though she was the last piece in the complex jigsaw puzzle that was his life, which he had not even realised was missing until he had found it hidden in the most unlikely of places.

His mouth was pressed into her hair now, kissing the top of her head, breathing in the essence of who she was, and as Kate turned within the circle of his arms she closed her eyes so that he could hold her and brush his lips across her forehead and temples.

'I am so sorry,' she choked out, and looked up into his face. 'You must think that I am totally pathetic, but the call was about Gemma. Oh, no,' she added quickly, when Simon gasped in alarm. 'She's fine. Or at least as fine as she ever will be.'

Kate shook her head and pressed her palm against his chest, sending delicious shivers through him. 'Tom has been called in to repeat some tests after his yearly checkup. He has a cold that won't go away, and she is terrified that his cancer has come back.'

'Oh, I am so sorry,' he murmured as gently as he could. 'Are you worried?'

Her answer was a short shrug. 'Not yet. I know that there is nothing I can do until the test results come back tomorrow, and all his other tests are fine, but I can't get that through to Gemma.' Kate gave a long sigh and waved her cell phone at him. 'A boy she likes at her special needs school made some jokey comment and she didn't know how to take it. She got upset. Then he got upset. Then the rest of the class got upset and before long the teacher had to call my dad.'

Kate closed her eyes and rested her head against the crook of Simon's shoulder.

'He didn't say anything insulting or unkind. Nothing like that at all! But she just didn't understand that he meant it as the kind of banter that we used to have. And it breaks my heart. Every. Single. Time. There are so many things that she will never love like we did. I just want her to be happy. And it's so hard.'

Simon groaned out loud. 'I am the one who should apologise. I have seen you all day and not once asked how Gemma is getting on. How old is she now? Twelve?'

Kate smiled as though the sun had come out again, and Simon's heart leapt at the intensity of joy in Kate's face. 'She'll be thirteen in three weeks' time, but she is already a teenager at heart—right down to the nail polish and fashion. I shall be working extra shifts at head office at this rate, to pay for all the designer labels that she will need to look cool in the next few years.'

Simon paused for a moment, before lowering his voice and asking, 'Is that why you agreed to take this assignment? So you could work sooner at headquarters and be closer to home?'

Kate laughed out loud and shifted back slightly, so that she could stroke his cheek with one finger.

'You always were too clever for your own good, Reynolds. Do you know that?' But then her laughter eased away. 'You're right. I sold my flat in London six months ago and moved back to live with dad and Gemma. It wasn't… Well, it wasn't working out very well for me.'

'Ah,' Simon replied with a knowing nod. 'Was that not working out because of some uncaring boyfriend? Or was it—' and at this he flashed his teeth in a pretend grimace '—a lazy husband who did not polish the silver to your exacting standards?'

Kate reared back, wide-eyed, and stared at him. 'Has all this African sun gone to your head? No, Simon. No husband, boyfriend, or, in case you were wondering, illegitimate children.' And then she smiled and shot him a cheeky glance. 'I would have told you if you had asked. And of course I don't need to ask *you* about children. What did you used to say?'

She lifted her chin, and to Simon's horror gave a very good impression of his normal speaking voice.

'The first five years are crucial to career development, darling. Family life must wait until there is a firm financial footing.'

Simon dropped his head onto his chest and groaned. 'Oh, no. Did I really sound so arrogant and pompous back then? I don't know how you put up with me.'

'Oh, it wasn't so bad. You did call me darling now and again, and of course it wouldn't have been half as much fun without you to keep me on my toes.'

He looked down at her and pursed his lips. 'Fun? What *can* you mean?'

'We made a good team. Having you around meant that I had to work that little bit harder to get top marks in every class. You would claw your way to the top, then I would knock you back into second again. Just to keep you busy, you understand. I knew how you hated to be bored.'

'Hah!' he snorted. 'So that was the reason! You need not have worried. It was never boring when you were around. Darling.'

He smiled into her eyes, and she into his, and as the sun set behind Simon's back the only sound was the soundtrack of nature which was playing in the background.

It was as though they had never been apart. She made him feel young, and so full of enthusiasm and fire and life and energy for what was to come. So innocent, in many ways. She was the only girl he had ever felt so easy and comfortable with. The only girl he had allowed to peek below his outside layer of confident bravado so that they could share their goals and dreams.

Kate had taken hold of his hands and was splaying out his fingers on the skirt of her dress, which was now only just visible in the fading sunset.

Her face was lit by the rays of the setting sun, and seemed to glow in the orange and pink-tinged light. Her blonde hair was a halo of gold, her skin like sheets of the finest softest silk. He took in every tiny detail of how she looked and what she was wearing, the beach and the tree… and at that moment he fell in love with Katie O'Neill all over again. If he had ever fallen out of love with her in the first place—which, if he was being honest, he knew was highly doubtful.

He never wanted this moment to end.

'Are you happy here, Simon?' she asked in a soft and tender voice. 'I have no idea what being a king means, but the people must respect you very much. You should be proud of that.'

'Grateful rather than proud. It's a real honour.' He could hardly see her hand now, but meshed his fingers between hers before answering. 'I *am* happy in so many ways, but it's the usual story. The more I do, the more I see what could be done. I will have the chance to give my ideas on how to build a better future for young men like Paul. But it's not going to be easy.'

'Do you have a…a wife or a girlfriend to support you?'

He shook his head with a grin. 'No one will put up with me like you did.'

'I'm sorry to hear that. Of course now you are going to be a tribal king of the village I expect the girls will come flooding around to take a look at you. Girls *and* their mothers! Speaking of which—and don't bite my head off—have you told your mother your news? I know that she would be very proud of you and what you have achieved.'

Simon inhaled slowly before answering in as calm a voice as he could manage. 'Actually, I *have* told her. We've met up a couple of times over these past few years, on my rare trips back to London, but only for coffee…maybe dinner. But this is different. The King has asked me to invite my family to the official coronation ceremony next weekend and, seeing as she is the only family I have left outside Africa, I asked her if she'd like to come and take her place as—well, sort of a village Queen Mother.'

He looked up and grinned into Kate's shocked face. 'I'm not sure that the village is ready for the Parisian couture hats, but she will be staying with me for a couple of weeks out in the wilds.'

'Your mother? Queen of the couture boutiques? Alone with you in the jungle? Oh, I would pay to see that.'

'Then why don't you stay, Katie? It would be great having the two of you in the village. They won't know which way to look first. A lovely blue-eyed blonde or a haughty aristocratic brunette. It could be great fun.'

'Fun?' Kate snorted with a harsh laugh. 'Oh, Simon. You have to be kidding. I won't be coming to your coronation, and I certainly don't want to meet your mother again any time soon.'

'Wait a minute,' Simon replied in a tight voice. 'I thought you got on well with my mother?'

'Oh, I did,' Kate said in an exasperated voice, and shook her head. 'Until she decided to have an affair with my widower dad while still being married to yours. I know…' She held up her hands in response to Simon's harsh cough. 'I know my dad was equally to blame. But have you any idea what it was like for him? He had been alone for so long, and then he met your mother. She was married, she was lonely, and he fell in love with her out of the blue. He didn't ask your mother to come into his life—she just did. And I know that neither of them could have predicted what happened. It just did. And then he had the cancer diagnosis and she dumped him.'

Kate shook her head from side to side, eyes closed, and her voice dropped into her shoes. 'She dumped him when he needed her, and he let her go without saying a word because he cared too much to make her stay and watch him suffer. I still can't forgive her for that. If you need someone to blame for me not coming with you, you can start there.'

Simon paused and gave a short chuckle.

'No, Katie, that's not fair. Tom is an adult. He could have dealt with his life and let you be free to live yours the way you wanted.'

'Oh, Simon. Don't you get it? It wasn't Tom I stayed for. I stayed behind for Gemma.'

'Gemma? I don't understand. She has a wonderful school for the deaf, and people to help her.'

'Yes, she does, but I was the only person in Gemma's life who stayed when the going got tough. Gemma really loved having you around, and then you were gone. She kept asking me where you were. Tom was having chemotherapy, and she was so terrified that he was going to die and leave us, like Mum had. Do you know that she still has panic attacks every time we pass the hospital where he was being treated? She couldn't go to school. I couldn't go to work. It was a nightmare!'

Simon sat back on the beach towel with a resigned thump. 'And Gemma asked you to help her get through this? Is that right?'

Kate nodded. 'She begged me to stay. She was so

terrified that I was going to leave her that she had to sleep in my bed for the next six months, so that she could wake up and realise that I was still alive and not going to walk out on her or die. On the day our mum died I promised Gemma that I would always be there for her. And that came before anything. Even you, Simon. Which was why I needed you so very badly.'

Kate clutched at Simon's arm, almost scrabbling at it with the intensity of making him understand what she was saying. 'I was so lonely. Tom and Gemma were depending on me, but who was there for *me*? That's why I needed you, Simon. I needed you more than I had ever needed anyone in my life before. And you weren't there. Not a message, a phone call, a postcard. Nothing. You cut us off as though we didn't exist any more. Have you any idea how painful that was? To be rejected—again! It doesn't get any easier, you know. Being rejected and abandoned isn't something you get used to.'

'Oh, you don't need to tell *me* about that. Don't you remember what it was like when my father left for yet another trip to Africa? We'd spent two years together before I even started uni, putting together the technology the villagers could use with help from volunteers, but that was never enough. He kept going back, and back, then back again. It was an obsession, and every single time he left he gave me the same speech about how I was wasting my time at university when I should be out here with him to make the project work. He might have sacrificed his business, but in the end it was his family he truly left behind.'

Kate knelt in front of Simon on the towel, so that she was looking up into his strong and loving face which was cracked with grief and confusion.

'I remember that you cared about him, and wanted him to be safe in Africa. That was why you were so angry at your mother and Tom for letting him down, when he was doing such amazing work here,' she whispered, taking his hands in hers and hoping that he would listen. 'I wasn't too happy about it myself. But you blamed *me* for bringing them together, and that wasn't fair, Simon. I was there when they tried to explain that neither of them expected to fall for each other. Do you remember? Tom certainly never saw it coming. I know that.'

Simon gave a brief nod and blinked before answering with a sigh, 'I know. You told me that my father was a coward for taking the easy way out, and that if I left I would be doing the same thing. Running away from the hard decisions.'

Kate winced. 'That was cruel of me. I am sorry for being so hard on you.'

Simon slipped a hand out of her grasp and reached up and stroked her face. Her eyelids fluttered half closed at the delicious sensation.

'Don't be sorry,' he said, in a low, tender voice. 'You were telling me the truth but I wasn't ready to hear it. I idolised my father and he was never there for me. Never. Do you know the real reason I went into maths and computing? It was so that he would be proud of me and we would have something to talk about when he came home. I think you were the only person who knew just how hard I worked to get his seal of approval.'

Simon choked on his words and slipped back on the towel, found something fascinating to look at on the beach stretched out in front of him.

'I think it was a case of facing up to the truth that my dad was not the perfect man I had built up in my mind over the years. Far from it. He loved his work here, and he devoted so much of his life and time to it he never once counted the cost for the family he left behind. Mum was lonely and Tom's a fine man. I don't blame her, and I am sorry that I blamed you for making it happen.'

Kate opened her eyes and stared Simon in the face. 'It's not the same. Call me hard and callous, but your mother abandoned Tom when he needed her.'

Then her voice changed, and when she spoke again there was a chill in her tone.

'And then you did the same to me. How could you do it? How could you walk out on me like that at the precise time when I needed you most? And then blame me for not going with you?'

CHAPTER SEVEN

KATE sat back on her heels and waited, hardly daring to breathe but desperate to finally hear Simon's reply. The silence stretched out between them, so that when he did speak his words seemed to echo around the cool night air and vibrate with the tension in his voice.

'The day of his funeral, I looked into that grave and I saw that all my efforts had been a worthless joke. I had lived my life striving to be the best in class so that he would pay me some attention, and there I was. A first-class honours degree. Graduating joint top of the class. And it meant absolutely nothing. The man I had worked so hard to please was gone. My mother had fallen for your dad and my family was gone for ever. I felt as though everything I had built my life on had been swept away by some giant landslide.'

The anguish in his words hit her like a physical blow. 'I wanted to be there for *you* when he died,' Kate said, desperate not to break the connection between them. 'That's why I decided to wait until a better time, when we could both think straight about how we should build a future together. I didn't have a second of doubt that we could do it. As a team. Me and you. Only you left before we could talk. And that's what hurt the most. The fact that you cut me off.'

His head dropped forward onto his chest and his fingers clutched onto Kate's, drawing her next to him. 'I didn't know who I was any more. And then I turned and looked at you,' he said, in a sweet voice with a gentle smile. 'You were standing next to me at the graveside. You *were* there for me. And I saw someone who put her family first, before herself—and still got the grades by working twice as hard as anyone else in the class. You wanted to work to give yourself a future. And it blew me away. That's when I knew that I had lost the sense of what I truly wanted in life. The old me was in that grave with my dad, and I had no clue what to do any more.'

Kate started to speak, but Simon's forefinger pressed against her lips to silence her. 'You're right. I did run away. I ran way to find myself. It was a selfish thing to do, but I knew that if I stayed I had nothing to give you or offer you. *Nothing.* No home, no money, and not even the job we had both worked so hard for. It was all gone. I can't even guess at how tough it must have been, but you had always been a fighter. Until that moment I don't think I fully realised just how much I had come to rely on you for my strength. I loved you, Katie. I loved you and I had not once told you that out loud.'

His eyes scanned her face as his fingertips brushed gently across her forehead and into her hair. 'So, you see, you were right to call me a coward. Telling you how I felt would have been a sign of weakness, and the Reynolds family did not *do* weakness.'

His laugh was hollow and bitter, and Kate shook her head in gentle agreement. 'Oh, Simon. I wish you had talked to me about what you wanted.'

'And said what? My dad had promised the village that he would finish the work he had started—they were relying on him! But I knew that was never going to happen. He was gone, and so was the finance. All I could offer the people was my time and my commitment to keeping the promises he had made.'

He dropped his head back and pressed both hands palm flat against the top of his head as he closed his eyes. 'I know you, Kate O'Neill. I knew that you would never leave Gemma—especially when your dad had cancer. And I had been to Ghana before. I *knew* there was no way you could have brought a child out here. Life was tough enough for a single man on his own. I just about coped with finding clean water and food to get by. A little girl like Gemma would have been…impossible to care for. And I was certainly in no state to be a father figure. No. You had to put her first. And that meant you had to stay. And I had to leave on my own. No matter how much it hurt.'

'Were you lonely?' she asked, after what was probably only a few seconds of silence which had seemed to stretch for hours.

He nodded. 'Missed you all like crazy. But somehow being in Ghana helped me mourn my father. This was the one place where my dad and I had been happy working together. The village gave me a home and a purpose in life. A lifeline, if you like, when I needed it. Everything I have done since then has been to repay that debt. They are my family, and now they are going to be my people.'

'You kept the promises your dad made. You should be proud of that.'

Simon smiled a couple of times. 'I suppose I did. Just

as you kept your promises to Gemma. And *you* should be proud of *that*.'

The light had faded now to a dim glow from the white sand, and as he smiled in reassurance Simon noticed the dark shadows that were growing all around them as the final rays of the sun dropped below the horizon, taking the glorious sunset with it.

Suddenly Kate rolled to one side, away from Simon, and in one movement started gathering together her things and tugging the dress she had borrowed from Molly back into position.

'What is it, Katie? Are you cold?' Simon asked.

'No. Not cold,' she replied, with a smile he could hear in her voice. 'Just sad.'

He reached out and caught her hand, forcing her to be still for a moment.

'Why sad? We've both come a long way these past three years so that we can sit on this beach together in this beautiful place. Who knows what the next three years will bring?'

'Oh, Simon. Don't do this. You are a prince, soon to be a king, with responsibilities and people who need you. Right here in Ghana. While I still have a sister back in England who needs me, and a dad who is sick. So not much seems to have changed on that front, does it? If anything, I would say that our lives are even further apart than ever.'

Simon gasped and choked out a question. 'You don't mean that? We have only just…'

'Just what? Remembered old times? Yes, it has been wonderful, and just for the record I never stopped missing you. But unless one of us is prepared to move to another continent this is one long-distance relationship that is not going to work. We both know what this kind of job does to couples.'

Simon took an even tighter grip on both of her hands.

'Don't give up on us quite just yet, Katie. You were always the creative one. Won't you even try to come up with a few ideas? Andy doesn't work here all year—far from it. And there are webcams and video links we could bring in, so that you could see your family and talk to them any time you wanted.'

She paused for a moment, then nodded. 'That's true. But it would have to work both ways, so that you could talk to the other tribal leaders from the UK. Here is an idea for you. From what I saw today you are proud of being a one-man band, taking all the responsibilities onto your own shoulders.' Kate slid closer to him along the beach towel. 'It doesn't have to be that way. Most of the other presentations today came from teams of volunteers, where the company has provided the equipment and there's more than one project leader.'

She reached out and touched his face with one finger before smiling at him. 'Maybe it is time for you to share the workload and forgive yourself a little. After all, you are Chief of Development. You could spend time raising funds and extra sponsorship back home and still...' Then she stopped and sighed. 'But you don't want that. Do you?'

He slowly shook his head from side to side. 'I am going to be the new king, with all the responsibilities that come with that honour. I can't leave my people without the support they need.'

'Then we are stuck, aren't we?' she answered, and

slowly slid her fingers from his grasp, breaking their connection. 'Perhaps we ought to get back in time for dinner, Simon?' Kate said, trying to keep her voice calm and light. 'Molly will be wondering where we have got to.'

And with that she turned away from Simon to gather up her shoulder bag, and waited for his reply—which never came.

The final touches of sunset were throwing deep shadows along the beach now, the red and scarlet bands adding texture and colour to a sky which seemed to go on for ever across the horizon. But under the trees the light was fading fast. The hotel lights shone ahead as a beacon, and lanterns had been hung in the palm frond pagodas along the edge of the shore, but Kate was struggling to see Simon's face.

Something had changed in the air between them, as though the light under their easy camaraderie had just been extinguished.

'Can you find your own way back?' Simon finally asked, in a low voice full of concern but distant and cold as the night air.

Simon was still sitting with his arms resting on his knees, staring out towards the horizon. She could not see his eyes at all now, but she knew. She had made a mistake. And this one was not going to go away.

Her own way back? No, she did not want to find her own way back.

She wanted to dance along the moonlit shore, with Simon holding her hand like he used to. She wanted to skip in and out of the waves and laugh so hard that her stomach ached.

She wanted him to want to be with her. But that was impossible.

'Don't worry about me,' she replied. 'I've made it on my own this far. I don't need anyone to show me the way.'

And with that she set off back down the beach alone, grateful for the cover of darkness so that nobody would see her fresh tears.

CHAPTER EIGHT

'HEY—guess what the airport shuttle just delivered?'

Molly Evans strolled into the sunlit hotel breakfast room, dragging behind her a battered-looking trolley suitcase, that was looking very sorry for itself.

Kate dropped her coffee cup with a clatter and knelt down to fling her arms around the dirty bag. 'You made it with only hours to spare! Oh, I am so glad to see you, old pal.'

She gave a contented sigh before sliding it closer and grabbing the handle. 'The bliss of having working clothes for the field trips! I don't think these girls would last long out there. Do you?'

Molly and Kate both looked down at Kate's shoes as she sat down and stretched out her legs. Her very high platform court shoes might have come from a famous French show-maker, but they both burst out laughing at the horror of what Kate would probably be wading through during her project trials.

'Good point,' Molly replied with a grin. 'But they certainly worked their magic. These last few days have been terrific—thanks, Kate.'

And then Molly stepped forward and gave Kate a warm hug. 'You were fantastic, and I know that Andy will be thrilled at the feedback. I confess Prince Simon did help with the media coverage of the event, but you will be pleased to know that four new corporate sponsors are interested in his pilot study. So, job done.'

'Thank *you*, Molly,' Kate replied, and blew out a sigh of relief. 'It has certainly been an eventful few days.'

Then Molly looked from side to side, to check that nobody was close enough to hear what they were saying, rubbed her hands together, and sat down opposite Kate at the breakfast table, propping her elbows next to the juice and toast.

'Now,' she whispered, and leant across the table, 'onto far more important things. How are you and Simon getting on?'

Kate opened her mouth, then closed it again. 'Oh, Simon. He did give an excellent presentation, and the solar energy…'

Molly waved her fingers across the table and hissed, 'I don't mean about work—although he was totally brilliant—I meant *you* and Simon.' And Molly raised her eyebrows several times.

Kate took one look at Molly's face, groaned, and dropped her head into her hands. 'Oh, no. Was it that obvious?'

'Totally. I know Simon, and the fact that you couldn't keep your eyes off each other sort of gave the game away.'

'We couldn't?' Kate whimpered.

Molly shuffled in her chair like a schoolgirl anxious for gossip. 'So tell me everything. When are you coming back? Or is it Simon's turn to visit you? I am dying to know. You do make a very handsome couple.'

Kate swallowed down a gulp of coffee and looked over her cup at Molly. 'Sorry. Not going to happen. We both have too many other people to think about.'

Her voice broke as she said the words, and she sniffed

away the burning in her throat as she reached out for more toast. Only Molly beat her to it, and laid her hand on top of Kate's.

'The last thing I need are two lovestruck people on my watch. Let's order more coffee. I want to know the whole story. Right from the start.'

Two hours later Kate stopped outside Simon's hotel room door, raised her hand, then lowered it again.

She was leaving this lovely conference hotel and heading out to see the two new projects that Andy had started. Which meant that it was time to say goodbye to Simon. There was no need to visit his village—the work there was well under way and all her questions had been answered. If she did go it would only be a feeble excuse to spend more time with Simon.

Of course she was tempted to stay. Simon was right. Modern communication technology meant that she could see and talk to Gemma every day if she wanted, even from rural Ghana, but there were so many other things to consider. And her head and heart were not co-operating very well. Perhaps these next few days on the road would help to clear her thoughts. She certainly hoped so.

Come on, Kate told herself. *You need to do this. You are a professional. It is a common courtesy to say goodbye to your client. Even if it is Simon.*

Every part of her heart was screaming *stay*, while her head was running through all the perfectly sensible and logical reasons why that was such a crazy idea, and she should run as far and as fast away from Simon as her legs and a fast plane could carry her.

She had held it together through a nightmare dinner, where they had only been seated three chairs apart, and then days of official presentations and speeches and reports. The conference had been a constant buzz of frenetic activity and deliberate business, designed to make certain that there was no time when she could be left alone with Simon to express a simple *Nice to see you again. Goodbye. Have a nice life, Your Majesty.*

As far as the other delegates were concerned she and Simon were simply work colleagues supporting an important local initiative.

This was how she wanted it. *Wasn't it?*

Shame that Molly and goodness knew who else had seen through her little charade.

But all she had to do was survive the next few minutes and then she could walk away and get on with her life. From now on their relationship would be totally professional, and conducted through the safety of an internet connection. If he could do that, then so could she.

So, before she could change her mind, Kate pressed the doorbell on Simon's room and instantly heard footsteps on the other side of the door.

He was wearing his old cargo trousers and T-shirt and looked about seventeen, but it was the expression on his face that took her breath away.

He was looking at her with such love, and with a smile so honest and open and real, that just being so close to him, so near and yet so far, was overwhelming.

'Hey. Everything all right?' he asked, scanning her face in concern. 'Sorry that things were so busy that we haven't had a chance to talk.'

He doesn't know. He doesn't know that I am leaving.

'Absolutely, but the conference has been a huge success.' She smiled politely, and then said what she had to say before he had a chance to answer or her nerve failed. 'Molly's waiting for me downstairs, but I wanted you to know that I heard back from Tom this morning.' She paused for a second, then smiled to reassure him. 'The last results came back as negative. It was a false alarm—he just has a bad head cold.'

She watched Simon's shoulders slump and relax, and then without hesitation he simply stepped forward and wrapped his arms around her in a delicious welcoming embrace of such love and warmth that it disarmed her. Every good intention she'd had of simply walking away from him fled out of the window.

'I'm so pleased for you... But did you say Molly was waiting? Does that mean you are heading out on your field trips?'

She nodded, incapable of speech.

His hand came up and pressed her head closer into his embrace. He drew her into the room and out of the empty corridor.

'Oh, Katie,' he whispered as his cheek moved against hers, filling her with the smell of him and hotel shower gel.

Kate rested her head on his shoulder. If she was ever going to say it, then this was the time to do it. 'The other night,' she whispered into his shirt, 'at the beach. When I told you that I had made my own way so far and didn't need anyone. That wasn't even close to being true.'

He turned his head just enough so that she could see the dust on his eyelashes and the huge dark pupils at the centre of the grey eyes which had entranced her from the first moment she had seen them all those years ago in the lecture theatre at university. The words she was about to say froze on her lips.

'I know. This is hard on both of us,' he said, his voice intense, almost a harsh whisper. 'Can I at least talk you into staying until my coronation?'

Kate slowly shook her head, and braved a closed-mouth smile before replying. 'Promotion will mean that

I can work full-time from home. I will be there to make Gemma's breakfast and spend every evening and weekend with her. Tom has done an amazing job over these last few years when I have been travelling, and he has never once complained, but he is due to retire next year and is ready for a rest. It's my turn, and I want to be there—no matter what his test results say.'

'I understand. You have to be there for Gemma and your dad. But the last few days have shown me that we have something amazing here, Katie—and don't even try to deny it. We could be happy together, and that usually does not come around twice.'

His fingers were on her forehead now, stroking her hair back from her face, and the pleasure was so heavenly that she could have died with the wonder of it. She longed for him to keep going. But she couldn't—not when she was so close to the knife-edge between leaving and staying. This time she had to be the strong one.

'You're right. I am still as crazy about you as I ever was. But things are so different now, Simon. You have your responsibilities to your people. I have my sister to think about, and we come as a two-for-the-price-of-one package deal. If I moved here so would Gemma, and we both know that would never work. It has taken years for us to find a perfect school for the deaf, and Gemma loves it there. Moving her away from her friends and studies at this stage would be way too traumatic. She needs that special help and I promised her that it was all going to be okay.'

He started to protest. 'No.' She pressed a fingertip to his lips. 'Please don't make it even worse. It is better for me to go with the knowledge that we still care about each other. That's something we can take with us wherever we go.'

His hands cupped her face as he leant in and kissed her with such gentleness and tenderness that she almost lost her nerve. It was if he was pouring every special memory of their life together into one kiss, and she sank into it with all of her heart.

It was the most wonderful kiss she had ever received, and she knew that she would never forget it.

And then her cell phone rang, and she pulled back and smiled, fighting off the tears as his fingers slid away from her skin, probably for the last time.

'That's probably Molly with my transport. She's arranged for me to spend two days doing field work out of town.' She paused and tried to form more words, but her mouth and throat were not co-operating. Instead she smiled and brushed her lips against his cheek, and fell into his arms, hugging him, embracing him, eyes pressed tight shut, desperate to capture how his touch felt so that she could remember how it felt to be loved in the cold winter days to come.

Seconds seem to last for as long as the years they had been apart, but finally Kate pushed herself away from his body and stood back on wobbly legs.

'You are going to make a wonderful King. I love you. And don't you dare forget that.'

She had done it. She had told him she loved him. And the words had been just as heavy and wooden and as awkward in her mouth as she had imagined they would be. Her pain and regret felt as exposed as if she had ripped open her chest and cut her heart out, then presented it to Simon on a platter crafted from her stubborn pride and sacrifice.

Before she could change her mind, Kate flung her bag over her shoulder, snatched the hotel room door open and ran away from the man she loved so very much. And it broke her heart all over again.

* * *

Simon stood on the balcony of his hotel suite until the Jeep carrying Kate away from him was nothing more than a hint of red dust in the air lifted by the old tyres.

Watching her load her bag into the boot and slump dejected into the passenger seat had been one of the hardest things he had done in a long time.

Molly and some of the conference delegates had come out of the hotel to see her off, and she'd waved farewell to them through the open window, smiling at their laughter, but he'd only had to catch a glimpse of her face to see that her heart was breaking as much as his.

Seeing Kate again had reminded him what it felt like to be with someone who knew you and loved you for yourself, despite your faults. And he had plenty of those. Oh, Katie. The only girlfriend he had ever truly loved.

How could he have been so selfish and blind to her needs, to the burdens that she had been carrying back then?

He had been so very, very selfish and self-centred. It was a wonder that she had stuck with him at all. And now she was gone.

He had to do something—anything—so he paced back and forth across the room before picking up the dossier he had worked on with Kate. On the front cover was a photograph Paul had taken of the new schoolroom they had built in his village. In the picture the children were crowded around Simon, chatting and eager for his attention. Their energy and enthusiasm seeped out from the image and helped him shed a little of his pain with the memory of the touch of each small hand in his. This was his life, captured in a small photo on the page of an official report.

He paused and pushed his hands deep into his trouser pockets, finding a few teeth-rotting sweets which would be snatched up with great joy by the children when he got back to the village later that day with his mother. Those children were future entrepreneurs and leaders in this wonderful country of people filled with big hearts and spirit—but it was going to take a lot of work and energy to help them get there.

His energy. His time. His work.

Simon's steps faltered. Was Kate right? Did it have to be all his own work? Was there any way he could achieve the same things with the help of other volunteers? Could he work smarter? He had trained gap-year students, college drop-outs and environmental scientists for years. Many of them came back to work on individual projects, but up until now it had been one sponsor and one project at a time.

In a few days he would be crowned King—perhaps it was time to show the village that they had been right to put their faith in him.

'Simon? Are you okay?'

Molly Evans appeared in the open doorway to his room. She had taken off her smart jacket and was dressed in a simple cool top and trousers. She looked about twenty years younger than he felt at that moment.

'I'm…' Then he stopped. 'No. I'm not okay. I'm losing Katie all over again—only this time she is the one doing the walking away.'

'Of course she is,' Molly replied in a totally matter-of-fact voice as she strolled onto the balcony. 'You can tell me not to interfere, but from what I've seen Kate loves you. She knows that she can't make a life with you without impacting your work as the new King or her family back in England. She's scared, Simon. Scared of losing you but also scared of what staying would mean.'

Then Molly smiled and added in a low voice, 'Every King needs his Queen. It's time to put all that expensive education to good use and come up with a plan. And it had better be a good one.'

Simon smiled back with a self-dismissive snort, then paused and nodded sharply towards Molly. 'You're right. It is time to get creative. And I have an idea. It's going to take a lot of work, and I am going to need your help to see it through.' And then he hit Molly with one of his killer smiles. 'This conference is not over yet.'

CHAPTER NINE

COMPARED to the green and lush world where she had spent the last two days, visiting dedicated and under-resourced project volunteers, the hard surfaces of the airport seemed a cold and unwelcome place.

Passengers of all shapes and sizes were shoving and pushing their way forward, trying to find the correct check-in desk for their flight or meeting up with friends and family.

She had never felt so startlingly bereft and alone.

The lights were too bright, and the clattering sounds of people and equipment and aircraft seemed deafening inside her head, creating a whirlwind of crashing sound.

She perched on the very end of a hard metal mesh bench, already crowded with several families and their assorted luggage, and hugged her precious suitcase even closer while she waited for her check-in desk to open. She was late, and the gate was later. But she had left it right until the very last minute before leaving for the airport. Hoping against hope that Simon would call her on her cell phone.

But he had not called. Why should he? She had made it clear that she did not see any future with him in Africa, and this was where his heart was now—not the rolling chalk hills of cold and green Hampshire, England.

Simon was gone. She had pushed him away with logic and common sense and practicalities. All because she had been too cowardly to fight against convention and persuade Simon and the wonderful, generous people she had met over the past few days that she and her family could have a new home here.

That had been a few short days ago—but not any more. *Ghana had worked its magic on her.*

As she'd tossed and turned in the stifling hot village accommodation she had been offered so generously by the project team, her mind had constantly come back time and again to Simon's challenge.

Perhaps Simon was right and this *was* a place where she could create a new life?

The more she thought about it, the more options seemed to spring up. Molly had emailed her details of the latest communication software the company were rolling out to the field operations and it was certainly impressive. The more she considered what her life would be like in the next five years, the more she wondered if living and working with Simon in Ghana could become a reality. Could she work part-time in Ghana and England? Andy had managed it for years. But could *her* family cope with that?

A single telephone call had been all that was needed. It had lasted hours, and probably cost the company more than she wanted to think about, but at the end of it both Tom and Gemma had agreed that her happiness was all they wanted. Gemma would love her to be home now and again, but she had always adored Simon, and any chance of a trip to Africa was a brilliant bonus—especially now that he was going to be a king.

She had never loved her family more.

To say that Andy had been thrilled that she wanted to apply for his job would be the understatement of the year!

In fact she'd had to rein him back and talk job-share and part-time. But that was next week's problem.

Anything to stop her heart melting at the memory of Simon's tender kisses.

Simon had always been her prince, and now he was going to be a real king, with his own people. The hard reality was that she was going to have to work hard to prove that she was up to the job of being his queen.

She had always thought of herself as Cinderella, making the fire for her stepsisters—or in her case her sister and stepdad. That was where she belonged, wasn't it? Not upstairs, sharing her life with a king.

Kate closed her eyes and tried to block out the noise. Perhaps she should risk the heat and head outside for an hour, to help relieve her headache? The check-in desk might be open by then. At least she would escape that strange drumming that was going on inside her head. Drumming and chanting and... Drumming?

Kate's eyes flew open just as the crowds of passengers seemed to part like the Red Sea before Moses, leaving a wide channel for a very strange procession which seemed to be focused on...*her*. Two drummers in bright striped skirts and bandanas jigged and jogged their way through the airport lounge towards her lowly metal bench, followed by a line of men and women in stunning togas, headdresses, and heavy golden necklaces and royal regalia.

Then she felt her eyes widen as two men in full ceremonial Ghanaian dress walked in a stately fashion towards her. One of them even dared to give her a wink, and gestured with his head over his shoulder as they got closer.

Startled, Kate blinked several times before she recognised that the handsome young Ghanaian was Paul, looking every inch the Prince in his splendid costume.

Hardly daring to breathe, Kate lifted her head and

looked over Paul's shoulder—into the pale grey eyes of Simon Reynolds.

And her heart sang.

He was wearing his tribal toga—a brightly coloured strip of woven cloth wrapped around his tall, athletic body, with the end thrown over one shoulder. A golden sash crossed his bare bronzed shoulder, and his lower arm was wrapped in a stunning amulet. To complete the picture, one of the boys she had seen on the photo of the village school was struggling to control the weight of a great fabric parasol and hold it over Simon's head.

On either side of Simon were royal attendants. The tall proud men each carried a golden ceremonial staff, topped with a large carved golden standard, and as she watched in stunned silence Simon turned slightly and whispered to one, then the other, before stepping forward so that he was right in front of her.

Kate looked into his smiling eyes and tried to express how totally confused and elated and stunned she was, but failed. It was all too much. He came to her rescue.

'I might be only a prince, not yet a king, but I come from a long line of proud people,' he said, his voice resonating around the airport, which seemed to have come to a universal halt while everyone found out what was going on and why there was a royal procession there.

He glanced to one side, and out of the corner of her eye Kate saw Molly giving him a supportive thumbs-up. 'A wise woman once said that every King needs his Queen. So I come to you today, Miss Kate O'Neill, and offer you my hand.' His eyes smiled, and she could see the edges of his mouth quiver with emotion. 'Will you do me the honour of being my future Queen? My partner? My wife? Will you share my life with me, Kate? Say yes. You have always been a princess in my eyes. Let me make you a queen I can share with the world.'

Somewhere in the airport an announcement was going out about the check-in desk for a flight to London, but Kate wasn't interested in that any longer.

All she could think about was this man in a toga, who was asking her to marry him before a crowd of strangers. All that mattered was Simon, his grey eyes fixed on her with such pleading and such love that the only thing she could do was smile and nod in reply, and keep on nodding until the doubt on his face was transformed into startling happiness and joy.

Then the drummers started banging away for all they were worth. Simon's friends from the village began dancing from side to side, their ceremonial staffs transformed into marching band batons, and the great parasol slid slowly to one side as its holder joined in the jig.

'You have always been my Prince, Simon Reynolds. I never thought you could one day be my King. We will find a way to make it work, because I don't want to spend one more miserable day away from you. That's why I applied for Andy's job yesterday.'

'You did?' he replied, his forehead so close to her. 'I've spent the last twenty-four hours convincing your company to build on what we have achieved so far and use us as a pilot study for similar initiatives all over the kingdom. They'll be sending a whole team of new graduates to make it happen. But I'll need you with me every step of the way to make it work. Say yes, Katie. My beautiful princess. My Katie. Say yes, so that I can take you home to begin our new life together.'

CHAPTER TEN

IT WAS a perfect morning in June, and the cathedral bells were ringing out across the old narrow lanes and university buildings of the ancient city which Kate now called her wet season home.

They were ringing for her, Kate O'Neill, and the man she was going to marry. When Simon had been crowned King of the village all she'd had to do was watch in wonder as the local tribal Kings and their families gathered in the huge Durbar Square. Simon and the elders had paraded around, greeting the hundreds and then the thousands of local inhabitants who had come to meet their new King.

Under the huge parasol, and again accompanied by the elders carrying tall staffs with golden standards, Simon had accepted the honour of having the crown placed onto his head with such dignity and gratitude that Kate had swallowed down tears of pride and happiness as he'd sworn allegiance to the principal King and been given his new name.

It had been a magical day. The crowning ceremony had been followed by feasts and wonderful food, then dancing late into the night—and music: music all day. Music so joyous and exuberant and full of life that just the memory of that day made her grin with pleasure.

It was memories like that which had sustained her over

the winter months and the weeks they had been apart as Andy and Molly had worked to create the new project programmes.

Sometimes it had felt as though she had dreamt the whole thing.

Simon—her Simon—was a king. A *king*!

A man other people loved and respected and went to for advice and decisions and help. She was so proud of him, but the more she thought about her new role, the more she sometimes felt intimidated by the enormity of her responsibilities.

It had truly hit home when she'd returned to the village with Tom and Gemma in the Easter holiday. It had come as quite a surprise when the village matchmaker had called on her father out of the blue with his attendants, to start negotiations for her marriage to their King. Traditional gifts had been offered, which she'd had to formally accept and examine with great detail before they could finally become officially engaged in the eyes of the community.

It was only then that it had seemed real. She was engaged. To a king.

Kate smiled to herself as she looked out onto the sunlit streets, then suddenly Gemma sneezed, and Kate looked up at her across the width of the limousine and smiled as Gemma rubbed her nose and grinned back at her.

Trust Gemma to bring her back down to earth.

Gemma had loved everything about Africa. The light, the colour and the atmosphere. And the villagers had taken her into their homes and their lives. The pretty blue-eyed girl with the lovely smile had already broken the hearts of several local boys, but there was only one person Gemma had wanted to be with and spend her day with—and that was Simon. She'd followed him to school, lip-reading his answers to her non-stop questions, helping out on the computers, sitting next to him at mealtimes and holding tight onto his hand when they'd been in the crowds of well-wishers and curious people.

Kate reached out and squeezed Gemma's hand for just a few seconds, and Gemma crinkled up her nose in reply and used sign language to say, 'You look so beautiful.' She waved her hands above her ears. 'Especially the head thing.'

Kate casually patted the diadem the hairdresser had pinned onto the chignon below her veil. The tiara had been a surprise gift from her future mother-in-law, and it was a precious vintage piece which had been passed down through the family. Simon had called it a peace of-fering, and perhaps it was, but it was also the closest thing to a crown that Kate had ever worn, and it felt and looked amazing.

'Oh, this old thing,' she replied to Gemma, and they grinned in secret code.

'A crown for a princess.' Tom laughed on the seat next to her, and pushed against her shoulder playfully, in the jacket of his new morning suit. 'My two girls look lovely. I am proud of you both.' And with that Tom O'Neill sniffed several times and took a moment to look out of the win-dow, trying to look casual, as though he did this every day of the week.

Kate's heart melted. 'Now, do *not* get me going,' she croaked. 'This make-up has taken hours to put on.' And then they all laughed, sharing a precious last moment in private as the car slowed and turned into the long drive that led down to the cathedral steps.

Molly had already texted her to say that the cathedral was full to bursting with dignitaries, friends, extended family, colleagues—and sixteen very special guests from a small village in Ghana, who had arrived with Simon a few days earlier for a Royal tour of the town and the local countryside and a small inspection of Kate and her home.

Television cameras were already placed to broadcast the wedding to the world.

In fact, the whole week had been a blur of things to be done and organised, with radio and TV interviews, and time with the local dignitaries and the royal party from Ghana.

Chaos had reigned in the O'Neill household. The wedding dress had come first, and then coping with the stress on Gemma and Tom, and meeting Simon's mother again. The stress had never seemed to end. She was so grateful that Simon had arrived to help.

And of course there was extra stress in that this was no ordinary wedding. This was a royal wedding! Complete with complicated rules of protocol and statesmanship and visiting diplomats and so many people that there had been times when Kate had had to remind herself that she was doing this for Simon.

It scarcely seemed possible that their great day had finally arrived.

And now the car was crawling to a stop. The sound of bells rang out louder and louder across the square, and she saw the crowds of well-wishers and the press gathered outside the cathedral entrance. Her will faltered just a little.

She did not want to let Simon down at the last minute by doing something wrong, or saying something stupid, or falling flat on her face on the steps in front of the TV cameras. Not with the world's media looking on.

'He is still Simon,' her dad said softly, and clasped hold of her hand as she gulped down her racing heart, fired by exhilaration and excitement. Kate looked into the face of the man who had given her and her sister a loving home, and wondered how he had known. 'He loves you,' Tom said. 'Always has and always will, no matter what you do or say, and that is all that matters, isn't it? Okay?'

Kate threw her arms around her dad, hugging him even tighter. 'Thanks. That's what I needed to know.'

Then the chauffeur was holding the door open. Gemma had already skipped out of the car, and was waiting patiently with Kate's bouquet of yellow roses, fragrant freesias and white frangipani, which Simon had sent over to the house the day before, after sending the local florist into raptures.

'Are you ready to tell Simon how much you care about him?' Tom asked and smiled, and Kate felt her shoulders relax a little as he hooked her arm over his. 'I think you have both waited long enough for this moment. Don't you?'

She managed a brief nod before turning to grin at Gemma, who was far too excited and impatient to wait any longer. And then Kate looked into her dad's face for a second, before straightening her back and lifting her chin.

In an instant Kate had stepped out of the car and was standing in the warm sunshine, looking up at the impressive grand old cathedral. She was surrounded by light and noise and the clamour of people cheering and bells ringing and the steady beat of African drums and hornpipes.

This ancient place must have seen some remarkable celebrations and ceremonies over the centuries—but surely none more unique than this very special wedding.

Two of the musicians from Simon's village were standing on either side of the huge carved stone entrance to the cathedral, each holding a cow horn and blowing into the end of the horn with swollen cheeks to create the most remarkable fanfare of music this cathedral had ever heard. Their necklaces and bright striped bandanas were somehow perfect in the bright June sunshine.

Suddenly a band of Ghanaian drummers and dancers

emerged from inside the cathedral, and as Kate and Tom approached they started dancing and singing with such joy that Kate's heart sang.

Then the ancient doors of the cathedral swung open, and with one final squeeze of her dad's hand Kate walked slowly into the majestic church. Far above her the organ played 'The Wedding March', and somehow the combination of drums and horn-playing and organ music came together to create a magical combination of traditional English and African wedding music.

The dancers from Simon's village were first in line, followed by the drummers, all dressed in brightly striped woven fabric, and the whole group danced and moved and shuffled into the long aisle of the church which stretched between the entrance and the altar.

The music soared higher and higher into the carved stone roof of the cathedral, blending with the organ sounds and echoing back into the church.

Then the pace of the music changed, and the horn players and drummers started to sound faster and louder, and on each side of the aisle people started swaying to the music with a joyous rhythm.

Gemma walked proudly in front of Kate, carrying a smaller version of her bouquet, her body swaying to the wonderful beat of the drums.

The congregation rose as one, shuffling chairs and benches, all attention focused on Gemma. It had taken a lot of persuasion to convince her that a white net floor-length skirt with a Ghanaian fabric belt was the perfect outfit for a teenage bridesmaid. But Kate needed only one bridesmaid, and this was Gemma's day almost as much as it was hers.

The emotion was almost too much for Kate to stand as the wave of music swelled around her.

Kate was grateful for her father's arm as she stepped slowly forward, and for the first time in her life she felt beautiful, loved, adored and admired.

She looked out through her flowing silk net veil and could see two tall, proud figures standing next to the altar in front of her.

The dancers and musicians parted to each side and there he was, the remarkable man who wanted her to be his bride, achingly resplendent in his royal robes. His toga was of the finest cloth, woven just for this occasion. The golden sash crossed his chest under the clothing, matching the rich gold amulets on his arms. The polished glittering metal reflected back coloured light from the huge stained-glass windows which brought a whole spectrum of colour and light into the stone walls.

His crown was black, with gold emblems, and standing next to him was the principal King of the village and his attendants, standing tall and proud with their golden standards, heavy necklaces and medallions. But it was Simon—her Simon—who shone brighter than anyone else.

His happy smile beamed out as Tom took the final steps towards the altar and placed her hand in Simon's, and who looked into her face with such love and happiness that it made her head spin with joy.

He claimed her as his own as the warm sun outside the cool stone building shone through the stained glass, as the organ music blended with the drums and hornpipes. He lifted her veil and sealed their marriage with a kiss so tender and loving that she knew more than at any other time in her life that she had made the right decision.

He was the King and she was his bride and they would make a new home together in Africa. This was the life she had longed for. This was the life she had promised herself over all the years of struggle and fear and doubt and regret.

It had all been worth it. She was ready to start her new life with the man she loved. Her husband and her King. It was time to begin the most exciting adventure of her life and she could hardly wait.

EPILOGUE

A SPECIAL report from the *Hampshire Times Magazine*:

A small African village welcomes its very special new Queen

Queen Kate O'Neill Reynolds might come from a small Hampshire village in England, but the computer scientist and her family now have a new home in Ghana.

In January this year her then fiancé Simon Reynolds was crowned King of a tribal kingdom after spending years building on the work started by his late father to establish a technology centre in the Volta region of Ghana.

When Kate and Simon married, in an extraordinary cathedral wedding in Hampshire in June, their very special guests included the village's paramount King and his entourage. They had been so impressed with Kate's dedication and commitment to their area that the King decided to bestow this unique honour on Mrs Reynolds.

Kate Reynolds then travelled to Ghana and was made Queen, before Kings, chiefs and elders from across Ghana, together with her father Tom, younger sister Gemma, and hundreds of citizens, colleagues and well-wishers.

In a tradition known as the Enstoolment Ceremony Queen Kate received blessings before being presented with her official tribal clothing—golden slippers, a very special Kente woven toga and a golden crown, before feasting and dancing late into the night in one of the largest celebrations to be held in the area for many years.

It is understood that Queen Kate has already begun her royal duties by working on a new school for handicapped children in the district.

* * * * *

Coming Next Month

Available October 11, 2011

You can find more information on upcoming Harlequin® titles, free excerpts and more at
www.HarlequinInsideRomance.com.

HRCNM0911

REQUEST YOUR FREE BOOKS!
2 FREE NOVELS PLUS 2 FREE GIFTS!

Harlequin

Romance

From the Heart, For the Heart

HRI1B

*Harlequin Romantic Suspense presents the latest book
in the scorching new* KELLEY LEGACY *miniseries
from best-loved veteran series author Carla Cassidy*

*Scandal is the name of the game as the Kelley family fights
to preserve their legacy, their hearts...and their lives.*

Read on for an excerpt from the fourth title
RANCHER UNDER COVER

*Available October 2011
from Harlequin Romantic Suspense*

"**W**ould you like a drink?" Caitlin asked as she walked to the minibar in the corner of the room. She felt as if she needed to chug a beer or two for courage.

"No, thanks. I'm not much of a drinking man," he replied.

She raised an eyebrow and looked at him curiously as she poured herself a glass of wine. "A ranch hand who doesn't enjoy a drink? I think maybe that's a first."

He smiled easily. "There was a six-month period in my life when I drank too much. I pulled myself out of the bottom of a bottle a little over seven years ago and I've never looked back."

"That's admirable, to know you have a problem and then fix it."

Those broad shoulders of his moved up and down in an easy shrug. "I don't know how admirable it was, all I knew at the time was that I had a choice to make between living and dying and I decided living was definitely more appealing."

She wanted to ask him what had happened preceding that six-month period that had plunged him into the bottom of the bottle, but she didn't want to know too much about him. Personal information might produce a false sense of intimacy that she didn't need, didn't want in her life.

"Please, sit down," she said, and gestured him to the table. She had never felt so on edge, so awkward in her life.

"After you," he replied.

She was aware of his gaze intensely focused on her as she rounded the table and sat in the chair, and she wanted to tell him to stop looking at her as if she were a delectable dessert he intended to savor later.

Watch Caitlin and Rhett's sensual saga unfold amidst the shocking, ripped-from-the-headlines drama of the Kelley Legacy miniseries in

RANCHER UNDER COVER

Available October 2011 only from Harlequin Romantic Suspense, wherever books are sold.

SPECIAL EDITION

Life, Love and Family

Look for
NEW YORK TIMES AND *USA TODAY*
BESTSELLING AUTHOR

KATHLEEN EAGLE

in October!

Recently released and wounded war vet
Cal Cougar is determined to start his recovery—
inside and out. There's no better place than the
Double D Ranch to begin the journey.
Cal discovers firsthand how extraordinary the
ranch really is when he meets a struggling single
mom and her very special child.

ONE BRAVE COWBOY,
available September 27 wherever books are sold!

www.Harlequin.com

USA TODAY bestselling author

Carol Marinelli

brings you her new romance

HEART OF THE DESERT

One searing kiss is all it takes for Georgie to know
Sheikh Prince Ibrahim is trouble....

But, trapped in the swirling sands, Georgie finally
surrenders to the brooding rebel prince—yet the
law of his land decrees that she can never
really be his....

Available October 2011.

Available only from Harlequin Presents®.

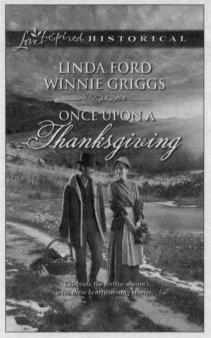